THE MISSING WIFE

*Mary Shelley Investigations
Book One*

Donna Gowland

SAPERE
BOOKS

To Kim

THE MISSING WIFE

Hope you enjoy it!

love,

Donna
x

Published by Sapere Books.

24 Trafalgar Road, Ilkley, LS29 8HH

saperebooks.com

ISBN: 978-0-85495-677-7

To my mum, Sylvia, and my daughters, Romilly and Zinnia

PROLOGUE

Claudine Lamont tied the straps of her hat below her chin and surveyed her features in the gilded mirror atop her dressing table. The shrunken cherubs danced and smiled around its rim, and Claudine smiled back at both them and her reflection. She hesitated, then slid the theatre ticket she had been holding into an old playbill, taking it out of the messy drawer, locking it and throwing the key out of the window. The gardener looked up at her in surprise, squinting in the sunlight. He picked up the key then looked back at his mistress. She nodded and turned away, concealing the playbill in the folds of her gown and brushing everything back into position. Claudine breathed in the fresh air of the early morning, and closed her eyes.

CHAPTER ONE

London, July 1814

'Our souls will not be parted…'

Mary Wollstonecraft Godwin was used to dramatic declarations of love masquerading as introductions, but Percy Shelley rarely accompanied them with a pistol. As he walked towards the dining table, the silver gun barrel reflected his wide eyes and unruly hair to the shocked Godwin family. Her sister Fanny giggled behind her napkin and their father's glare turned towards her, forcing her to clear her throat and feign civility.

'Percy, how lovely of you to join us… Papa, may I be excused momentarily?' Mary asked.

William Godwin narrowed his eyes, surveying the scene unfolding before looking down at his plate of untouched food. 'You may, Mary, but make haste about it. This mutton is cooling faster than his ardour…'

Fanny giggled again and Mary kicked her under the table, before pushing back her chair and walking over to Percy.

'Percy, what is the meaning of this?' Mary hissed as she took him by the elbow and ushered him out of the dining room.

'I have a plan, Mary. We shall never be parted again; we shall fall into the realm of those star-crossed lovers — Percy and Mary shall be Romeo and Juliet.'

Percy brandished a small glass bottle, its scratched label proclaiming the laudanum inside. 'Poison for you, pistol for me. We shall die as we have lived, for love.'

'Not before I have eaten my supper. Come on.'

Once she'd steered him outside into the garden and pushed the pistol back into his pocket, Mary allowed herself to be swept up in Percy's arms. For all his poetics and theatrical behaviour, there was a steel in his hold that melted her heart.

'A thousand stars could not shine as bright as my love for you, dear Mary.' He kissed her hand.

Mary frowned. 'Not one of your best lines; try not to include it in your next poem.'

The trees formed a cover around them, but a shard of lantern light slipped through the door. A sudden shadow obscuring the light told Mary that their time together had come to an end.

'Mary, return to the table, please.' Her father's voice was firm.

Percy held her close. 'Must you leave me? Each parting is a fresh wound.'

Mary smiled up at him. 'We have our plans and nothing and no one shall stop us; star-crossed lovers we shall be, tragic we shall not. Now, away with you, before Father brings out his whip.'

'Very well, I shall go.' Percy raked a hand through his hair. 'But I am counting down the days until our elopement.' He covered her face with light kisses that caressed her face like soft raindrops.

As Mary stepped back into the dining room, she was overwhelmed by a tremendous hunger. She resumed her seat and picked up her fork. Mr Godwin gestured for everyone else to do the same, but Mary could feel the heat of his disapproving gaze upon her as she cut into her meat. It could not, however, prevent her heart from thumping joyously like a loud drum. Though she half-listened to the conversation between Mr Godwin and her stepmother, Mary Jane, her thoughts — along with her heart — were with Percy. In two months' time, they would be together. In two months' time, they would leave Somers Town, and London would seem like a fog to them, a scarcely remembered thing, a footnote in the annals of a long life of love, adventure and travel. The world would open up to her like a precious shell, and the pearl of possibility would shine as a talisman. As a child, Mary's father had told her of the comet that had accompanied her birth, that it would guide her and keep her safe wherever she went. The celestial event had not prevented her mother's death shortly after her birth, but Mary hoped it would shine on her now.

CHAPTER TWO

Yawning deeply, Mary grabbed her scant possessions with one hand and her stepsister's hand with the other. Together they crept down the stairs, pausing as they reached the creaking step, waiting to see if it would give them away. When no noise came, Mary opened the front door and slipped out into the night, closing the door on the only life she had ever known.

'Isn't this exciting?' Jane said with wide-eyed enthusiasm, her dark curls coming loose from the bonnet as she hurried to keep up with Mary.

'Yes,' Mary said coldly, her face set with determination. She glanced back, beset by the terror of being seen or — worse — of being stopped. Two months of planning could all come to nothing if Mr Godwin caught wind of their elopement before she and Percy had even left London. Jane's continual chatter was distracting; Mary wanted to focus on reaching the corner of Hatton Gardens, where they would meet Percy and take the coach to Dover. If they made the first coach of the day, it would give them the advantage of a couple of days should Mr Godwin decide to follow them. She hadn't planned on bringing Jane, and hoped that her stepsister joining them on the journey wouldn't hinder Percy's enthusiasm. She'd had no choice. Jane had all but threatened to put a stop to the plans if she wasn't allowed to be a part of them. Better to keep her with them and on side, Mary had decided. The sky was dark, and the stone buildings looked intimidating under its black cloak. London seemed to hide ghosts at every corner, in every passageway. Mary felt exposed, as if she were being watched or followed; but every time she swung around to look, there was no one there, nothing but her own guilt and superstitious nature.

'It is no good. I cannot leave like this,' she blurted.

Jane, just a year younger than Mary, stopped and turned to face her.

'You cannot mean that! If you do not leave with Percy, his heart will be broken, and there is nothing worse for a poet than a broken heart.'

'In that assumption you are wrong, Jane. A broken heart is the stock-in-trade of a poet, and a talented poet is all the better for having received one. But you misunderstand me; I have no intention of abandoning Percy.'

Was it Mary's imagination, or had Jane's shoulders sunk a little then? It was of no import. She needed Jane to go to him, to have the carriage wait while she made right what must be repaired.

'We have little time; the sun is rising...'

'All the better to speed me along. I'll run all the way. Keep my bag with you and tell Percy that I will return in ten minutes.'

Mary didn't wait for Jane's response, turning on her heel and running back up the road that moments earlier had been filled with shadows. Freed of the baggage, her steps were swift. She was relieved to see the curtains of the house in Somers Town were drawn, the occupants still asleep. Mary quietly opened the door, slipped off her shoes, and made her way to her father's study. Inside, she opened his desk, extracted a sheet of paper, and poured her heart into a letter, her tears mixing with the ink as she signed her name at the bottom. Placing it into an envelope, she crept up the stairs to her father's bedroom and propped the letter against his dressing table. Resisting the urge to lay a hand on her beloved father's back and listen to his gentle snores, she froze at the sound of footsteps outside the door. Holding her breath, she sighed as the footsteps moved away. After a couple of anxious minutes, Mary tiptoed towards the door, crossed the landing, and made her way back down the stairs.

Outside, the sun had opened a lazy eye, flooding the sky with orange and pink. Mary rubbed her face, fatigue and disappointment setting in; now she had assuaged the guilt of leaving without an explanation or a goodbye, fear that she might have missed the coach to Dover took its place. Taking a deep breath, she ran into the sunrise, uttering a quiet prayer that she would not miss the coach under her breath.

She arrived just in time to see the last of the bags being strapped to the top of the horse-drawn coach. Percy and Jane were already seated inside the carriage, Jane's face a picture of serene smugness at her proximity to Percy. His appearance was one of composed civility, though his eyes darted around urgently, looking for her. When he saw her, he pushed past Jane, leaping out of the carriage and enveloping Mary in a tight embrace that took her breath away.

'Oh, thank goodness, I thought your courage had failed … or you had changed your mind.'

'Did Jane not tell you where I went?' Mary looked at Jane, who turned her gaze away, staring out of the window on the other side.

'She said something,' Percy replied, bundling her into the carriage, 'but I was so consumed by fear that I could not hear her words.'

'Everybody ready?' the driver asked with a sniff, not waiting for an answer before pulling on the reins and steering the horses into action.

The coach pulled away, tipping a nod back to London as the horses' hooves clattered on the cobbled street. A solitary magpie flew past the window and up into the sky, into a dawn of warm pink and purple which bounced against the grey of the buildings, illuminating the façades with a rosy glow. Mary's heart swelled at the beauty of the city, its quiet dignity that had for so many years mirrored her own. It was hard to leave behind. If she closed her eyes, she could smell the sweet aromas of early summer, the early morning dew, the flowers ripe with pollen, the day fresh with possibilities. She felt the warmth of Percy's hand sliding atop hers. Mary opened her eyes and entwined their fingers.

'Happy?' he asked.

Mary smiled. 'I feel as if I am on the precipice of the very happiest of times.'

Twelve hours later, Mary's stomach churned and her head ached, her earlier light-heartedness replaced with a rising nausea that accompanied each jolt of the carriage. Though she had pleaded with Percy to ask the driver to make a stop, they had only done so briefly — more to rest the horses than the exhausted passengers. Jane had not stopped talking during the journey and seemed to suffer none of the ill effects of the perpetual motion of the coach. Mary had long since been content for Jane to monopolise Percy's attention, concentrating as she was on containing her nausea. It had left little space for poetry, philosophy or romance. No, she thought, let Jane be educated on Rousseau and Coleridge.

'I think I shall hire us a fishing boat at Dover. We will hasten our arrival in Calais if we are not encumbered by the shipping schedule,' said Percy now.

Mary did not have the energy or fortitude to complain, simply nodding, nestling herself into the crook of his arm and allowing her thoughts to drift, far ahead of timetables and dusty journeys, away from cold cemeteries or cold parents. Mary's future would be as bright as the evening sun that was streaming into the carriage, warming her face and soothing her temples as she closed her eyes.

'Do you suppose Fanny was much chagrined at being left behind?' asked Jane, her voice breaking into Mary's slumber.

It had never occurred to Mary to bring her older stepsister Fanny; truth be told, she wouldn't have brought Jane without the threat of blackmail, but the thought of Fanny left alone with Mr Godwin and Mary Jane, in a house without Mary's even temper and Jane's exuberance to counterbalance their moods, stirred a fresh guilt. Putting herself in Fanny's place made Mary see again the impulsiveness of her actions; her father's face swam before her eyes, frowning with disapproval. Mary swallowed down the bile that rose again in her throat; it was too much to contemplate.

'I think I am going to be sick,' she spluttered.

'Stop the coach!' Percy pounded on the roof. The horses' hooves came to an abrupt halt. Mary barged past Jane, propelling her body forward until she emptied her stomach onto a patch of grass at the side of the road.

'Mary!' Jane scolded, putting a handkerchief to her nose and turning her head away from the smell.

'Have you any water? Is there anything to drink?' Mary's throat was scratchy and dry.

'Not unless you want to share with the horse,' replied the driver, picking his nose and flicking it in front of him. Mary's stomach turned again.

'I have this…' Percy held out a hipflask.

'What is it?' Mary asked, trying to sound more worldly than her sixteen years.

'Gin.'

Mary shivered. Gin brought to mind Hogarth's *Gin Lane*, with its tumbling babies and mothers with loose clothing and even looser morals. Even so, she took the flask to her lips, tossed her head back and gargled the spirit, spitting it out on top of the vomit.

'What a waste of good liquor.' The driver shook his head.

'How much longer to Dover?' Mary asked.

'Almost there.' The driver pointed. In the distance, the port of Dover's white cliffs hazily punctured the skyline, and the bustle of activity replaced the slow countryside they had crossed through.

'And I can get a fishing boat over there, you say?' said Percy.

'Yes, at the dockside.'

Mary steadied herself for hours of waiting about, shivering on the docks while Percy tried to strike a deal. He wasn't a natural haggler, and she couldn't offer any guidance in financial matters, having almost no experience of money at all. Percy's substantial family wealth was matched, so far as she could tell, only by his ability to spend money on any flight of fancy.

By the time they reached the port, night had thrown a blanket over the sky, the dark shadows only disturbed by the orange glow of oil lamps and men busy handling fish and manoeuvring boats. Mary and Jane huddled together, united in their discomfort. Percy, oblivious, blundered on, casting a bohemian shadow as he weaved in and out of docking ports, and spoke to various men who shook their heads or scratched their beards. This went on until a sharp whistle filled the air and Percy gestured for Mary and Jane to follow him. Hidden behind a sailing vessel was a small wooden boat, like a shelled pea.

'Surely you cannot expect us to sail in that?' Jane said with a snort. 'We will drown before we have left the harbour.'

'Jane, let us take whatever we can — we cannot afford to waste any more time.' Mary rubbed her temples.

'If you prefer, we can leave you here for the evening. I am sure these fine gentlemen would be happy to entertain a pretty young woman,' Percy added.

Even in the darkness, Mary could see the blush that rushed to Jane's cheeks. She knew how Percy's good-humoured words would ignite the quiet spark for him that Jane did not bother to hide, even if he did not know it himself.

'Well, I suppose the sea looks calm enough, and it might be romantic to be on the high seas on a summer's night...'

Whatever else Mary thought about her stepsister, there was no doubting her flair for the dramatic.

'That's the spirit, Jane.' Percy squeezed Jane's shoulder.

Mary felt jealousy twisting in her stomach like a worm. She forced herself to smile.

'Mary, are you ready for a poetry recital on the high seas?' Percy asked.

'Absolutely,' she replied through gritted teeth.

True to his word, Percy shivered through poem after poem, no matter how much resistance the sea put up. As the sky darkened and their route to Calais became a darker stab into the unknown, Percy's enthusiasm was not dampened by the huge waves and the thunderous storms that punctuated each stanza, attempting to drown out his words. Mary winced and curled up in the boat's foot, but it offered little defence against the cold waves which crashed over the bow. Somewhere between the two lands, her eyelids drooped and her spirits sank lower.

'Is this not invigorating?' Percy punched the air, and Mary was gripped by a momentary impulse to return the gesture to him.

'I fear Mary's seasickness is overpowering her senses, Percy. Perhaps some Shakespeare might soothe her?' said Jane.

'*The Tempest*? It was made for such circumstances…'

Mary half opened an eye and caught the look of the fisherman in charge of the boat, his features screwed up with confusion. He must consider them a league of oddities, she thought. Such cares would normally bother her, but she would have to get used to being an outsider, a curiosity; that was par for the course when eloping with a married poet. The moon cast a ghostly reflection in the water and, for a moment, Mary saw her father's disapproving face looking back at her. It seemed to float on the surface before dissolving — another reminder of all she had left behind. Percy's words roared in her ears, accompanied by Jane's overenthusiastic clapping.

'*Encore! Encore!*' Jane shouted.

Mary's temples throbbed; she wished for nothing but silence and firm land.

'Tell me more about Paris, Percy,' said Jane excitedly.

Mary rolled her eyes, turning away from the incessant chatter. She had no need of his words; they were nothing more than an appropriation of her own mother's. For Mary, the journey to Paris was a pilgrimage, a way of getting to know the woman she had never known by following in her footsteps, seeing the streets with the same fierce wonder, her heart swelling with the same political stirrings. For now, though, only the stirrings of her stomach could claim her attention and she turned her mind to rest. Her body stopped fighting the undulations of the tide and used it as a rhythm in the way she had been taught as a child to count sheep when sleep evaded her. Sleep crept over her like a slow mist, pushing on her limbs until she felt as heavy as a log. Even Percy and Jane had quietened; the early hour had overpowered them all, charming them into precious rest.

Mary saw herself running through the woodland by her house, her yellow dress matching the brilliant daffodils that filled the parks. A bright sun dripped in the sky, liquifying the clouds and blazing on the ground in front of her. In the dream, a sudden dark cloud appeared, rain falling like water from a jug. She opened her eyes to see a wave curling over the side of the boat, rushing towards her. The wood beneath her feet was too sodden to get purchase, and she slipped as she tried to clamber upright. Percy rushed towards her, throwing himself into the arms of the wave, adding his drenched body to hers. The wave retreated.

'Mary, are you all right?'

Her teeth chattered too much to answer him.

'You are drenched!' It was Jane, calling to her from the other side of the boat, untouched by the wave and dry.

Percy continued to hold Mary to him, transferring his dampness onto her.

'Take those clothes off or you will catch a chill before we land at Calais.'

Mary shook her head, water droplets shooting off in all directions.

'What would be the point? The wind will blow the clothes into the water or, if it does not calm, there will only be more waves…' She brushed down her wet skirt and regretted it.

'Something else? From your case?'

'And have that ruined too?' Knowing Percy, he'd have her swap clothes with the boatman or arrive in Calais wearing nothing but her undergarments. Having left a trail of scandal in her wake, she had no desire to start a fresh one before she had even stepped ashore.

'The wind is picking up,' she said. 'The sun will rise soon and by the time we arrive in Calais, I will be dry. Dishevelled, but dry.'

'And every bit as lovely.' Percy took her hand and kissed it. The spark that ignited from his touch warmed her body and spirits.

'There are fishing nets there, if you are feeling the chill.'

'No, thank you.' Mary shuddered at the idea of landing in Calais like a prize catch. 'Calais is not so very far away,' she said, hoping she was right.

No more sleep came, nor did she seek it. Instead, she rested in Percy's arms. Jane had fallen asleep and soon the dark unrest was replaced by calm waters and the sweet birdsong that chorused in the air. As the day broke, new possibilities shone on the horizon and thoughts of England and her life there were swept away. When they blew into the harbour at Calais, a bright, clear sky greeted them.

'See, Mary, how even the sky welcomes us?' Percy said with a smile, his eyes shining. He pulled her to him, but as he tightened his grip, water dripped from her dress.

The fishing boat was moored into place and the fisherman gave Jane his arm and helped her from the boat. When he offered Mary his hand she shook her head, her cheeks flaring with shame at the sorry sight that she must look, her hair stuck fast to her head like seaweed, her dress wet and heavy like an umbrella — it was hardly the sophisticated impression she had hoped to present. Still, there was time to remedy that, and a new place would give her the opportunity, without the whispers and judgements of London.

'Is it not wonderful, Mary? Is the air not so fresh?'

She knew well the expression that danced over Jane's face; it was the first burst of enrapture that would last only until they journeyed to another place. Like a magpie, Jane would always be swayed by a new, shiny jewel and would have no compunction about stealing it from another's nest. Mary breathed in the air, her nostrils reporting nothing more than salt, sand and the overwhelming stench of fish — perhaps hers wasn't a romantic sensibility after all.

'It is clear and bright, as you say.'

They stepped onto the pier, their portmanteau behind them in the arms of the boatsmen. Percy's face shone like a pearl, showing nothing of the ravages of their sea journey. Mary did not need a mirror to know that she wore each league of the journey like scars.

Percy took Mary's arm, stepping her out of Jane's brisk pace. 'I have booked us rooms at Dessin's,' he said.

Mary frowned. 'Dessin's?'

'Yes!' Percy hopped like a happy toad. 'We shall start our travels in the style in which we mean to proceed, in comfort and love.'

His eyes shone with an intention that needed no deduction. It was the same passion that had almost overcome him as they had sat on the bench in the graveyard, surveying the centuries of silence and paying tribute to her mother's grave. If he could be overwhelmed by ardour in places of stone and death, then a place bustling with life would surely make him combust with desire.

'I have booked two suites, one for Mr and Mrs Shelley — for those are our true names, the names of our heart, though I despise the society that makes us wear those hateful conventions like shackles…' He frowned and looked out to sea. 'And one for Jane, of course.' A mischievous grin spread across his face. 'I have asked for her room to be apart from ours, so there may be no…' He paused. Mary knew he was searching for the word with the correct iambic pentameter and truth. 'Interruptions,' he said at last.

'It will be luxury enough to sleep in a bed and not on a drenched boat.'

'I shall walk ahead and announce us.'

Percy strode past, signalling for the luggage to keep pace with him. Mary fell into step with Jane again.

'Percy is jovial this morning.' A note of suspicion laced Jane's voice.

'Yes, travel and adventure are most appealing to him. I expect for one with such liberal and philosophical tendencies, the freedom of travel is the only way to live.'

'Did I overhear him say that we would stay at Dessin's?' Jane's eyes widened. 'Dessins is famous…'

'Yes, and we are infamous, or at least, if we are not yet, we soon will be. Oh, Jane, how could Percy take rooms at a hotel inhabited by every wealthy traveller? There will be more English aristocrats here than in the London theatres. How are we to remain inconspicuous?'

Mary clamped her mouth shut; lack of sleep had loosened her tongue. It did not pay to be so unguarded around Jane; she could see her sister's mind memorising the details, her taking a quill and writing the words, sharpening their points until they were able to wound their target. As Mary spoke, Jane's expression had become blank, as she weighed up whose side to be on for this battle.

'Mary.' Jane put a hand on her shoulder in feigned sympathy. 'If you are to live an authentic life with Percy, you must renounce society's rules … as your mother did.'

Jane's words fell like a blow. She knew where to aim. The insinuation that she was not good enough to be Percy's true equal was one thing, but to compare her to her own mother and to find her wanting was something else entirely.

Jane walked on ahead, her back straight and her head held high. Mary fought the urge to rush up to Jane and push her into the water. The thought lightened her spirits as they continued towards the pier end, where Percy waited. As their eyes met, Mary knew that the mischievous glint in his eyes mirrored her own. That was all that mattered. Jane was nothing more than an annoying fly; she was to be tolerated or ignored.

The Hotel Dessin dominated the shoreline, its patrician façade mimicking the golden sand. Though it was not yet high season, it was busy enough and workers darted between canopied tables where women sat in expensive lace outfits, fanning themselves and sipping tea from bone china. Percy brushed a hand through his hair and dusted down his outfit. Mary and Jane did the same, though Mary's cheeks burned at the thought of the patrons tutting at each streak of seawater or patch of sand dried onto her dress. They walked through to the reception area, where a young luggage porter struggled to keep upright a golden trolley loaded with heavy portmanteaus and trunks. Mary scanned the faces of the patrons, but none were familiar to her. She breathed a sigh of relief, then joined Percy at the reception desk.

'Your visitor arrived a little earlier…' the man at the desk told them.

Mary and Jane looked at each other, each besieged by a sinking feeling.

'Visitor?' Percy kept his voice even.

'Yes,' the man said. 'She is over there.'

He pointed to an area to the left of the desk, overshadowed by the arms of a large palm tree. The figure sitting underneath it wore an elaborate hat and held a bag in front of her stomach as if shielding herself from the other patrons. There was only one woman in the world Mary knew who held a bag like that.

'Hello, Mary Jane.'

Mary stepped towards her stepmother, putting her cheek to hers and planting the weakest of kisses on it. The kiss was not reciprocated. Mary Jane's lips were a straight, unimpressed line.

'This is an unexpected...' Percy paused. 'This is unexpected. Is Mr Godwin with you?'

Mary's heart quickened and she suddenly felt lightheaded. She reached out towards the wall to steady herself.

'My father, he is not ... here?'

'To draw more attention to our shame?' Mary Jane hissed through gritted teeth. 'This is a private matter which does not require a public audience.'

'Rooms...' Percy murmured, turning towards the desk where the reception clerk was watching the scene with interest. 'I will locate our rooms.'

'An apartment suite on the ground floor,' said the man, handing a key to Percy. 'And the other room is on the second floor.' Percy swept the second key from him.

'We will find it.'

'Your luggage will be brought up by the porter.'

'Come along, Mama.' Jane swept Mary Jane along, trying to engage her in polite conversation in an attempt to diffuse the current situation. 'Mary and I shall show you to our suite. Mr Shelley is to take the other room on the second floor. Is that not correct, Mr Shelley?'

Mary and Percy shared a look of relief at Jane's quick thinking.

'Yes, of course, that is to be the arrangement.'

Mary Jane pulled her bag closer to her. 'Well, at least that will go a little way to squashing the whispers of a harem.'

'A harem?' Mary shrieked. The busy hum of activity in the reception area stopped. If their arrival had not heralded attention before, it did now. 'How can people talk such nonsense and actually believe it?'

Mary Jane's hands shook as beads of sweat appeared on her forehead. 'We will talk about this in the suite. We will not fuel idle tittle-tattle.'

Mary recognised well the fury contained behind her stepmother's blank expression, that cold demeanour that revealed nothing yet said everything. Not for the first time did she wonder how her father could have married a woman like Mary Jane after knowing her mother. Mary Wollstonecraft had been a philosopher, writer and advocate of educational and social equality for women. Mary Jane had nothing to offer but stoicism and flattery. How could her father have been so susceptible to it? They were as different in looks, manners and viewpoint as stone and air.

The walk to the suite was short, but as Percy went to step into the room, Mary Jane blocked his way, shaking her head.

'Perhaps you would make yourself comfortable in your own rooms, Mr Shelley. We will call on you when we have concluded our affairs here.'

Mary saw Percy's shoulders drop as he turned away, all signs of his previous vigour gone.

Mary Jane closed the door and turned back towards the sisters as they sat down together on the sofa.

'Are you not ashamed of this public display of debauchery? Have you no mind of the damage you are doing to your prospects?'

'Prospects?' Mary asked, stiffening.

Mary Jane stretched out a long finger towards her. 'I am not talking about *your* prospects. You have none. Your betrayal surprises no one, Mary.' Her voice shook with anger, and her face had taken on a purple hue. 'I speak only to Jane. Your father knows you are a lost cause.'

'A lost cause?' Mary repeated faintly. 'My father thinks me to be a lost cause?'

'You are determined to follow the path set by your mother.' Mary Jane shrugged. 'And we all know where that will lead.'

The note she had left for her father had done nothing to soothe him, Mary thought. Knowing that there was nothing she could say or do to make peace with him gave her a feeling of weightlessness, as if she had untied the final familial cord. Without it, she felt unanchored.

'We will collect your belongings, Jane, and we will sail home together. I booked two tickets for the voyage, so it will seem like nothing more than the adventure of a mother and a daughter. Then we can pretend that this brief interlude never happened.'

Jane nodded and went to stand, but Mary pulled her back down.

'No, Jane, you must not return with her. There is nothing for you in London except a life devoid of excitement and adventure. Nothing but monotonous days of sewing and reading until you make a suitable match. Where is your revolutionary zeal?'

Mary swallowed. Though she had disliked the idea of Jane accompanying them, she was determined to prevent her sister from returning to their old life when so much more lay in front of them on this dazzling horizon. Jane bit her lip and clutched Mary's hand.

'I know there is merit to what you say, but how can I jeopardise my future?'

Mary Jane took off her hat and pushed back the hair slicked to her forehead, her impassive expression slipping into one of smug satisfaction.

'I am pleased that you are showing good sense, Jane. Now, let us retrieve your luggage and we will make our way home. You have been missed.'

Jane nodded. Mary Jane re-positioned her hat and smacked her hands together.

'Now that is settled, I have a tremendous thirst for tea. I will secure a table in the fresh air. Mary, you may join us, if you wish.'

Mary had no wish to join them. 'That is very kind, but I will find Percy and inform him of the change in plans.'

'I do hope it will not prove too much of an inconvenience to him. Though I am sure that behind his poetic foppery there is a small measure of sense ... if not propriety.'

A knock at the door broke the tension, and Mary rushed over to open it. The young porter who had been pushing the golden trolley in reception stood before them with arms full to bursting.

'We will deal with this, Mary.'

Mary nodded. As she walked down the corridor, she heard the loud thud of trunks hitting the floor and Mary Jane's exasperated moans. At least she had something else to occupy her anger. Her mind raced through all the things her stepmother had said, the casual cruelties that dripped off her tongue and landed so sharply. Flying up the staircase, she tried to recall the number of the second room, but could only remember the floor. It was of no matter, for as she raced up the stairs Percy was racing down them. His face, as it beheld hers, was a bright candle in a dark room.

'Mary, oh, Mary.'

He waited until a grand woman clothed in a silk dress that hissed as she walked was comfortably out of sight before rushing to envelop her in his arms.

'What is happening?' he asked, his hands stroking her hair.

'My stepmother has persuaded Jane to go back to London. It seems she has already taken the trouble to purchase the passage, so it will appear as if Jane were never a part of our adventure at all.'

Percy stepped back, watching her face. 'And Jane, has she been so easily persuaded?'

'She put up no defence at all.' Mary sighed. 'I had expected her to have shown more mettle.'

'But she cannot leave! Without her, this is just another elopement, and I feel sure that once my grandfather hears of it my pitiful allowance will be severed entirely — and then, sweet Mary, how shall we live? We will find ourselves in a debtors' prison or some other hell before we know it.'

Mary raised her eyebrows. Percy had never mentioned this when he had spoken of their plan to leave England in his letters. Those lines had been pure poetry and fire; this new speech dampened her spirits.

'I had not realised that Jane was so important to you.' Tears pricked at her eyes. She was dirty and exhausted. 'Perhaps we should all cut our losses and return to London?'

Percy swept her up in his arms, whirling her around until the lights in the crystal chandelier above merged with the cream and green walls. He was the only man she had ever known that could change her mood with a single gesture.

'Mary, Mary, Mary. We must go to Paris and walk by the Seine, smell the jasmine of the Tuileries, watch the sun set behind Notre-Dame. We must follow in the steps of our ancestors and bring their words to life. I cannot do it alone. You are my soul's breath. Do not abandon hope now. Do not leave your Percy all alone.'

His gaze held hers. A fire burnt in his eyes, igniting her spirit.

'They are retrieving her luggage now and taking the Packet Service this evening.'

'Is there no persuading Jane to stay?'

Mary shook her head. 'My words held no sway. But then, mine are not as florid as yours. I appealed to her reason, but you ... you can appeal to her soul.'

'Then I shall take her for a walk while you keep Mary Jane entertained.'

They stepped outside into a cool and bright day. Mary Jane had sought a table shaded by a large oak tree that perched self-consciously at the edge of the hotel, as if aware of being out of place on the white shoreline. Percy straightened his shoulders, walked up to Jane and whisked her away before Mary Jane could utter any protest. Mary slid into the seat recently vacated by her sister and smiled innocently at the expression of shock on Mary Jane's face.

'Oh, tea,' she exclaimed, pouring herself a cup as Mary Jane's expression cooled.

'You know what they are saying about you in London?' Mary Jane sipped her tea, not taking her eyes from Mary. 'They say that you have bewitched him, that you are a witch and a whore.'

'I am a good many things and will be many things more, but I have none of those talents.'

'Harriet Shelley is writing letters to anyone who will listen, and you know that when there are rumours in the air, they spread through society like a wildfire.'

'Rumours, speculations, theories — are they not all bedfellows? Or, at the very least cousins?' What was that Shakespeare line about having a battle of wits but the opponent being unarmed? A fierce protective instinct dominated her, as if she had reclaimed her soul and purpose after Mary Jane's stark reminders of the small ideas that populated the city she had left behind.

'Do you not feel any sorrow for Harriet? Abandoned by her husband, left alone with a child and another on the way.'

Mary bit her lip. It was fine to think of their actions philosophically, even ideologically, but what of the human cost? It weighed heavily on her conscience, but any doubts she had fostered regarding Percy's wife had always been swept away by his enthusiasm and promises that his love for Harriet had been nothing more than a childish infatuation compared to the inferno of his passion for her.

'That is regrettable.'

'Regrettable?' Mary Jane snorted. 'This whole sorry business is regrettable. Perhaps in a couple of years when you find yourself in the same predicament, then you will see the truth of the matter.'

Mary reddened; these were thoughts that she too had considered. Mary Jane was still talking.

'She is also saying that your father sold his daughters to pay off his debts. Can you imagine the damage this is doing to his reputation? To Fanny's?'

Mary sipped the tea, keeping her hands underneath the cup to stop them from trembling.

'It has never been our intention to hurt or hinder anyone…' she replied.

'Intention or not, it is the outcome. Oh, thank goodness.'

A smiling Percy and Jane walked towards them; Jane's face glowed and jealousy knotted in Mary's stomach.

'Come along, Jane. There is no time to waste if we are to be ready for our departure.'

Jane shook her head and folded her arms. 'No, Mama, I shall not be returning with you. I am staying here with Mary and Percy. I have no desire to return to London at present, but thank you for your concern. It has been good to see you.'

Mary Jane's mouth opened and closed several times.

'You are staying here with them?' The words were laced with anger and disappointment.

'Yes, I am.'

'But what shall I tell Mr Godwin?'

'You shall extend to him the same offer I extend to all of my family: that you are most welcome to visit us and to keep in touch.'

Mary Jane crumpled in her seat. It was clear to Mary that she had no fight left in her.

'Very well.' She stood up carefully, as if uncertain of her ability to hold herself together. 'I shall … go for a walk before departure.'

'Shall I come with you?' Jane asked.

'No.' Mary Jane's voice was quiet, uncertain. 'I will walk alone, gather my thoughts…'

They watched as Mary Jane straightened herself up, using her parasol as a crutch, putting one uncertain foot in front of the other. Within a minute, she had blended in with the other women on the shoreline.

'Monsieur?' A polite cough drew their attention back to the table. The waiter presented Percy with a bill.

'What hypocrisy to talk about morals and then leave you with the bill,' Mary said with a tut.

'I have recently advanced your father a loan for a higher amount; a *tisane de thé* is nothing.'

Mary's heart pounded. How could her father send Mary Jane here to talk of morals and respectability when he was using Percy as a banker? The double standards were staggering.

'Let us return to say goodbye. At least then we can be sure she gets on the boat.'

Percy laughed, pulling Mary to him in a hug from which she extracted herself, then cupped his face in her hands and kissed him on the lips. She knew that the eyes of the other patrons would be on them, but she didn't care. Confused at first by the sudden, public passion, Percy's kiss was tentative in its response, but soon it met Mary's with the same ardour and enthusiasm, making her feel as if she were floating on air.

As the sky became heavy with dusky pinks and purples, they waved the ship away, the three of them huddled together as the lonely figure of Mary Jane, watching them like a masthead, receded into the distance. Mary breathed out; she knew that all chances of reconciliation with her father sailed away with that ship.

CHAPTER THREE

'Do you suppose we will be this season's prime tourist attraction in every place we visit?' Jane asked the following morning.

'No,' Mary said, though Mary Jane's brief arrival and departure had brought unexpected scrutiny. 'I would like to think that when we reach Paris, they will be quite disinterested in us. Everyone is bohemian in Paris, unlike Calais, which is why we are drawing such attention.'

'I feel like an object in a display case,' Jane said with a sigh.

'Do you regret staying?' Mary's heart quickened with a curious fusion of excitement at being free of Jane and panic that, without her, the gossamer-thin veil of respectability would be irretrievably lost.

'No, I do not. How could I have missed out on such an adventure? Notoriety is much more exciting than convention, do you not agree?'

They laughed with a camaraderie they rarely shared. Ordinarily, there was too much rivalry between them — albeit unspoken — for them to engage in meaningful conversation or have a relationship with the sort of depth that Mary was sure she would have had with her own mother had she lived.

Mary yawned and gazed across the shoreline, heavily populated with children flying brightly coloured kites and boatsmen wiping the sweat from their foreheads. 'I think I will go for a walk.'

'Do you want me to accompany you?' Jane squinted against the sun.

'No, Percy will be back soon. One of us should be here to see how he got on.'

'Surely the travel arrangements have been made by now? We have encountered so many setbacks.'

'He has his heart set on August in Paris.' Mary shrugged and turned to walk down the beach. As she approached the pier, she stopped to look at the boats, casting her gaze to the busy fishermen tying knots, casting nets and grappling with unruly fish. Their colourful language pierced the air, but was ignored by the well-to-do patrons who were oblivious to anything or anyone that spoilt their scenic view. The heat sizzled the pier's iron railings, and the seagulls hopped from foot to foot. Percy's outline appeared through the heat like a mirage. Mary stopped and waved at him; he waved enthusiastically in response, his arms outstretched as if drowning and calling for help. Something about it made her shiver.

'Have I been away for such a long time? It seems like I have.'

'The ocean of Time has transformed each minute into a wave of years,' Mary said with a sigh.

'That is a good line.' Percy kissed her on the cheek. 'I must use that in one of my verses.'

They linked arms and walked back towards the hotel.

'I have some good news and some bad news. Which shall you hear first?'

'The bad, then that will make the good seem all the better.'

'I have secured our travel to Paris, but it cost more than I had expected. When we arrive in Paris, I will have to secure more funds.'

'Will your father raise your allowance?'

Percy slapped his thigh uproariously. 'Give more funds? If he had his way, my father would cut me off without a penny! No, we cannot scavenge for funds from his affections; we shall be sorely disappointed.'

'Then what shall we do?'

'I do not know, yet.' Percy pulled Mary close and kissed her tenderly on the forehead. 'Something will present itself, I am sure of it.'

'If that is the bad news, what is the good news?'

'We shall arrive in style!' Percy gestured towards a vehicle waiting for them at the edge of the shoreline.

The carriage hired by Percy was grander than those that had ferried them so far and Mary relaxed into the journey, barely noticing the landscape as it rolled by outside the carriage window. She was still hazy with the fatigue that had accompanied her from Dover. Jane and Percy chatted incessantly and though Mary caught fragments of the conversation, she felt little compulsion to take part. Now and then, the carriage slowed, before the crack of the driver's whip spurred the horses into action again.

'We will rest in Boulogne for the evening,' Percy said as he nudged her awake.

Mary sat up and stretched. It was typical that just as she was finally getting some rest, it should be disturbed by Percy informing her that they were stopping to rest. Now her reverie was broken, she doubted she would easily find it again, but that wasn't Percy's fault. She smiled at him gratefully.

'We are taking rooms at the Château de Saint-Cloud.'

'That sounds terribly grand,' Mary said, ignoring the little voice that was totting up their expenses as they travelled.

'I believe Byron stayed there two summers ago,' Percy continued, his eyes aglow at the mention of the notorious poet in whose footsteps he was planting his own.

'Well, if the rooms are suitable for Lord Byron, then they are perfect for the future Sir Percy Bysshe Shelley.' Jane winked at Mary, who didn't need to look at Percy's face to know that he was beaming at the comparison with the elder poet.

'What is the time?' Mary asked with a yawn. 'My stomach is telling me it is time to eat, but my limbs are telling me it is time for bed.'

'It is time for both. But first…' Percy reached out a hand to help her out of the chaise.

'Oh my!'

Mary was ill-prepared for the vision that awaited her: the wide pavements nestled in the hillsides, the lake carved into the rich green scenery, the ducks and swans serenely swimming atop it alongside occasional rowing boats carrying people into the low, pink sunset. Something in the serenity of the vista reminded her of Somers Town, though they were quite opposite in appearance. Her heart suddenly ached at the thought of what she had left behind.

As if reading the melancholy in her face, Percy said, 'Let us retire to our rooms.'

'Yes, let's,' said Jane. She and Percy raced ahead, leaving Mary to follow in their wake.

The château was set back from the lake, shielded from prying eyes by a cluster of poplar trees. As they arrived, a woman was closing the wooden shutters in the upstairs windows, which made the house seem like it was closing one sleepy eye after another. The woman stopped and watched them as they approached, then she called back over her shoulder to some unseen person and the grand wooden door opened before they could knock.

Percy nodded to Mary and Jane and stepped through the door, conversing in his thickly accented French. The long journey had taken its toll on his ability to conjugate verbs. His failure to join the auxiliary of *être* to the verb *arriver* made Mary wince — it was good to know that her intellect was still sharp even when her mind wasn't. Eventually, after much misunderstanding from both the English and French parties, an *entente cordiale* was reached, and they were given the keys to their rooms.

'Shall we retire to the same room this evening?' Percy asked Mary quietly.

Mary, whose thoughts were chiefly preoccupied by a hunger for food rather than passion, shook her head.

'We agreed we will live as husband and wife in Paris. Until then, we must stick to our original plan.'

Percy shuffled his feet. 'I think you make excuses, Mary. Do you not want to be alone with me right now? Have our stolen moments quashed your passion?'

Mary hushed him. 'I am so weary from our journey. I had not realised I would be so tired. My mother did not mention traveller's fatigue in her journals.'

'Perhaps she feared the reality of travel would not match the fairytale of the public's imagination. They want illusion, not dirt and despair.'

Percy closed his eyes. When he opened them again, he looked startled. Mary turned to see what had caused his reaction. It was the woman they had seen closing the shutters in the upstairs windows. She descended the stairs slowly, her features small in a head which was disproportionately large for her body. Looking past them as if they were ghosts, her gaze halted, with a disapproving glare, on a servant. Sharp, abrasive words fell from her lips like shards of glass, each one pricking at the young woman, who nodded at each barked instruction before scuttling off.

'Marie will see to your supper now, sir,' the woman said, turning to Percy.

They were ushered through to a room at the back of the house where candles lit the walls from ornate gold sconces and velvet cushions adorned the seats. Mary tugged at the dress she'd worn since Calais, wrinkling her nose at the salty, damp smell and wondering if the other one had finally dried. Jane exhibited no such anguish, though her own dress betrayed the same streaks and stains as hers.

Goblets were placed before them, and were swiftly filled with claret, which Percy drank like water. Plates of food followed, served on silver trays which caught the light of the candles and offered tantalising glimpses of the delights aboard them. Exotic foods Mary hardly recognised, and couldn't name, followed, each superseded by something grander until a pig's head with an apple in its mouth provided the meat for the main part of their meal.

'That poor pig looks like how I feel,' Percy joked. 'Perhaps I shall write an ode about it. I have no interest in eating it.'

'And how would it begin?' Jane asked with a smile, the claret and candlelight bringing a becoming blush to her cheeks.

Mary, still fighting the desperate urge for sleep, saw all too plainly Percy's renewed enthusiasm for her sister. Susceptible to flattery at the best of times, flattery on top of a fine wine and a full stomach was practically seduction for him, she thought, pursing her lips before tearing at a hunk of bread.

'Now, let me see…' he started, scratching at his temple.

'Oh, precious pig, oh golden sow,

How we adore your visage now,

A shame to feast upon your brow —'

'How I wish you were a cow?' Mary suggested. Jane erupted into laughter, and Percy pouted.

'I think my Mary means to mock me. Do you think me bereft of talent, Mary?'

'No, no, of course not, Percy. You know I think you are the most exciting poet in England. I am sorry if I offended —'

'Percy, can't you see that Mary is fatigued, and it is making her exceptionally grumpy?' Jane interrupted. 'Observe her face; is her expression not like that of the sow? Save for the apple in its mouth?'

Mary opened her mouth, affecting the same blank expression as the poor pig on the table. Percy's mood instantly brightened.

'Now you have mentioned it, there is a slight resemblance in the lip's downturn.'

Percy tipped his glass towards Mary, his eyes shining in the glare of the candlelight, the claret awakening his senses and appetites.

'Mary, have you energy enough for a moonlit stroll?'

Jane sighed deeply, then stuffed a piece of bread into her mouth.

'Yes, our supper has renewed my senses and I feel infinitely more alert.'

'Infinitely?'

'Yes, infinitely.' Mary put down her napkin. 'Shall we go?'

CHAPTER FOUR

The following morning everyone's spirits were restored and even the horses at the front of the carriage neighed with a fresh vigour, matched by their enthusiastic pace. Mary could only imagine the scenery, encased as they were in the wooden tomb of the chaise. Only the increasing heat confirmed the passage of time, and Mary's enthusiasm battled with her fatigue.

Some hours later, the vehicle stopped to allow the horses to rest and the occupants to stretch their legs. It had parked by a patch of land away from the track, in a secluded spot shaded by thin trees that seemed to whistle as the wind blew through them.

'Are you still suffering with the heat, Mary?' Percy asked as he wrapped an arm around her.

'Yes.' She wiped her brow. 'I am unaccustomed to it.'

'There is a lake over there. Perhaps you might like to bathe?'

Mary looked towards the brown, turbid water. It wasn't the sort of lake to inspire confidence or spontaneity.

'Bathe?' She feigned ignorance of his intentions. He was a poet whose worlds comprised woodland nymphs who discarded their clothes to tempt weary travellers. Mary, on the other hand, found it hard to shrug off the cloak of respectability she had always worn.

'It is easy, Mary; you just take off your clothes.' Percy's eyes flashed.

'But the driver, the horses…' she stammered, heat rushing to her cheeks.

'The driver has the horses to attend to and the horses cannot articulate any judgement, even if they should feel it.'

'No,' Mary said firmly. 'I am too sticky to peel away my clothes.'

No sooner had she spoken than the naked, lily-white figure of Jane swept past her and splashed into the lake. Percy laughed and cheered as she bobbed up and down in the water, not seeming to care about being seen. Even the birds tweeted their approval.

'Oh, dear goodness, Jane, please get out of that water! You might catch cholera!'

'It is invigorating, Mary. You should try it.'

Mary turned her head away. She couldn't help but think such antics were sure to do nothing to counteract the rumours of impropriety. A rush of movement made Mary turn to see Percy running past, his buttocks wobbling freely like a pair of blanched oranges. The driver laughed and pointed at him, but Mary seemed to be the only one concerned by such things. She sighed and put her hand over her eyes. Percy joined Jane in the lake, and they started throwing water at each other like two frolicking children, each sending great waves covering — for a short while — the modesty of the other before each twisted their body back into the spotlight and offered a bigger, more dramatic splash than the preceding one.

'Are you sure you will not join us?' Percy encouraged.

The driver caught Mary's eye and raised his eyebrows.

'I will not be getting in that water, and I am outraged that you are both making such an exhibition of yourselves!'

'You sound like Mama,' Jane scoffed, punctuating the words by splashing water in Mary's direction.

Mary scowled, a cold fury dampening her spirits and hardening her resolve. She folded her arms and turned away from them. Nothing and no one would induce her to join in with this charade, and she resented Percy for even suggesting it. Typical of Jane to do anything to win his favour; Mary believed that there was nothing she wouldn't do if it gave her the advantage and made Mary seem dull and plain. And yet, heat quickened at her throat as an idea took hold — *could* she do it?

The driver had turned his attention back to the horses, whose manes were slick with sweat — he would think it nothing more than the foolishness of English people. Her fear that the daughter of Mary Wollstonecraft should be found in such an uncivilised state was merely her own. There were no parents, ties or societal bonds to keep her in place and Percy and Jane were splashing about as if they did not have a care in the world.

She reached to untie her bonnet, taking the first step towards liberation. Percy and Jane stopped splashing each other and waltzed instead, Percy taking Jane into his arms with the water as chaperone, its polite waves creating a parental distance between them. Mary's hand hovered over the button at the top of her dress, and she hesitated as she squinted into the water. The air had changed. Whereas the scene before had been childish and innocent, now that Percy held Jane close to him, it was infused with a fresh aroma. There was nothing between them, and their bodies — always kept at a distance — were close, too close for Mary's liking. Percy's swelling enthusiasm and the gaze Jane returned to him could light fires without kindling. Mary strode into the water, the bottom of her dress spreading out like an ink stain.

'That is quite enough of that. We will never get to Paris if we carry on with this tomfoolery.'

She grabbed Jane by the arm, who looked at her but offered no resistance to being dragged out of the water. Jealousy beat a thick and constant drum in Mary's body; her hands shook with it. Percy stepped back, sitting in the water and watching Mary. Even the horses had turned to watch the spectacle. Mary's cheeks burned as the sound of the driver's laughter bounced around the trees.

'Come along, Percy, we want to arrive in Paris before supper.'

Mary knew her tone was that of a chiding mother, but if it masked the bitterness and jealousy beneath, it was a small price to pay. Percy — who prized freedom and liberation above all else — would think very little of such a public display of envy, and Mary wanted to extinguish whatever spark she had witnessed between him and Jane before it engulfed their own.

Jane cut a shrunken figure as she trudged back to her clothes, her shoulders stooped, one arm slung across her breasts. *Too late for modesty now*, Mary thought to herself. Jane stepped back into her clothes and, in a quiet voice, requested Mary's help.

'You should have come in, Mary; it was most cooling to the senses.'

Mary bit her lip. *Cooling?* she thought. *It has done little but enhance them.* She discarded the thoughts; now was not the time for animosity. Mary envied Jane's ability to shed convention so easily, but now that her initial jealousy had cooled, a protective instinct took over, a sudden fear of what levels of impropriety Jane was capable of and how little thought she had of consequence. Percy paced around them, taking Jane's gaze with him. Mary lowered her own, determined not to be stung by jealousy again.

'Is this not a beautiful place, ladies?' He closed his eyes and breathed in deeply. Mary was relieved that his pleasure reflected no hint of her own ill humour. He kissed her cheek, and that small reassurance restored her equanimity.

'It is exquisite,' Jane agreed. 'Can we not make a home here, by this lake?'

Mary looked at her and smiled. 'Have you not said the same thing about each place we have stopped in?'

'Well, each has been beautiful. I would happily make a home in any of them.'

'And to think, we have not yet reached Paris. I fear you may combust at all the beauty there!'

Percy's eye caught Mary's, and they shared a knowing smile at Jane's unworldliness. Although Mary's own experiences had only been lived through the words of others, they were her mother's words and her heritage, which gave her a legitimate claim to them. Travel and adventure were her birthright.

With Percy and Jane dressed and the bottom of Mary's dress drying quickly in the sunshine, they made their way back to the coach.

'Did you enjoy your dip in the lake?' The driver chewed straw as he spoke to Jane.

'Yes, it was a nice way to cool off in this heat.'

'Me and the horses might join you next time.'

Jane's eyes widened and her face fell in horror. Mary could not help but feel a smug satisfaction. Actions had consequences, and though Jane might have felt like she did not have a care in the world when she was splashing about without her clothes, the eyes of the world had not left her for a minute. It was a sobering reminder for them all.

CHAPTER FIVE

It was late afternoon by the time they arrived at the Hotel de Vienne, where the dust from the wide roads had swept up and clung to the stone façade of the building. With none of the grace of the previous château, it was a little more out of the way than Mary had expected.

'Where exactly are we?' she asked.

The driver met her gaze with bemusement. 'Marais. This is a good place to stay.'

He dumped the luggage in front of them, tipped his hat and crashed the horses away like a highwayman, disappearing into the night with a greater speed than he'd managed on their journey.

'This is not Paris.' Jane pouted, her nose wrinkling in disgust at the sights before her.

'Of course it is. We are just on the outskirts,' replied Percy.

Everything was painted in muted palettes of cream and brown. The small trees that wound their way across the street were skeletal branches, offering nothing more than scorched patches of arid leaves. The overall impression it created, Mary thought, was more desert than thriving city. Even the air felt dry.

'We have finally landed in Paris, Mrs Shelley.' Percy squeezed her hand expectantly.

Mary blushed. So, this was where their true union began. They were out of the reproaches and restrictions of England and in a bohemian city that shared their values, would permit their passions and not judge them. Excitement tempered by nervousness crept slowly up her body like ivy. Now there were no obstacles to their union, they would be bound in body and soul.

'Can we eat? Will we have supper?' Jane asked.

'Yes, of course. I shall arrange our rooms first.'

'We shall walk around the hotel and get our bearings.' Mary placed her hand on Percy's, a small gesture of promise.

'Come along, Mary.' Jane linked Mary's arm and together they walked past the hotel's dusty façade, past the stone-cobbled area in front of it, and towards the small patch of garden hidden at the hotel's rear, where they sat on a wooden bench.

'You are so lucky, Mary.' Jane's cool voice matched her expression. 'To have the adoration of a great poet. You will be immortal.'

'I will not be immortal. No one is.'

'No, I do not speak of flesh and blood; I talk of souls and words that will linger on the tongues of lovers for centuries to come.'

'I doubt our words will last beyond our earthly lives, Jane.'

'But a poet…' Jane sighed. 'I can only imagine how it feels to be loved by a poet, to be wanted by a poet.'

You were wanted by him this afternoon. The memory crept into Mary's mind like an unwanted visitor. *You know exactly how it feels.*

'Will you promise me something, Mary?' Jane fidgeted as she spoke. 'Will you tell me what it is like? What I can expect? All I know is what has been written, and I doubt that tells the woman's story…'

The thought of sharing intimate details with anyone, let alone someone who shared the same aim, was disagreeable to her, but Mary patted Jane's hand.

'I'm sure all will be well,' she said simply.

The hazy figure of Percy stepped into the dusk, his radiance illuminating their pale surroundings. Mary took a deep breath, her heart pounding at the thought of the evening that lay ahead. She closed her eyes, allowing herself to fall into the exquisite trance of passion and desire. When she opened them again, she was ready.

Some hours later, after they had enjoyed a supper of fruit, cheeses and bread, accompanied by more than a customary amount of wine to quell Mary's nerves, Jane stretched, yawned theatrically, and announced herself as being ready to retire.

'Mary, are you ready for sleep?' Percy asked, his tone threaded with hope.

'I have consumed too much cheese to settle,' Mary replied, and Percy sighed. 'But I will feel much revived if we go for a moonlit stroll first. Jane and I discovered a pleasant garden before. While it will be no match for the Tuileries, it will ready me for slumber.'

Mary knew all too well Percy's predilection for the outdoors; he seemed to be roused by stone and statue. A stroll around the gardens would be just the sort of aphrodisiac to bewitch him.

'A walk would be beauteous.'

Jane made her excuses and left the dining room while Percy and Mary made their way outside.

After the stifling heat of the day, a breeze that made Mary stop and pull her shawl closer was most welcome. She looked up at the moon, which appeared to have taken on an icy glaze. Everything had changed; her entire life had rotated on an axis and she found herself plunging into Percy's world, as if diving into a bottomless ocean.

'The moon is so beautiful tonight; it hurts to see it so,' said Percy.

'Why does it hurt? Surely its beauty can do nothing to wound you.'

'No, but its temperance can. The moon is a witness to our bridal night, Mary. I feel a terrible judgement from its waxy eye. I worry I cannot live up to such beauty.'

He paused, staring fully at the moon with the pained expression of a spurned lover. Percy, usually so confident and full of life, had cracked open like a conker, his vulnerability more alluring to Mary than any moonlight.

'This moon may wane, Percy, but my love will not. My love for you is the very rhythm of my life. Each heartbeat affirms it and repeats it.'

Mary stood in front of him, the moon casting an ethereal glow that turned her skin to ivory. Percy looked upon her as if she were Pygmalion brought to life; her sculpted words silenced his own.

'You have elevated my soul to ecstasies I'd thought mere fancies of the imagination.'

He kissed her, his lips firm and dry with a hint of wine on his tongue. Mary steadied herself by wrapping her arms around him and then, when she was sure that she would not fall, she allowed herself to melt into the kiss, fragments of her former life floating from her like autumn leaves until she felt as light as the air, as beautiful and as full as the moon.

'Tell me, Mary,' Percy said as the kiss reached its natural end. 'Tell me all your dreams so I may guard and cherish them as my own.'

She linked her arm through his and they stepped through the garden. The moonlight spared no light for the trees, and she gripped his arm with sudden terror as a bat flew past their heads. Mary jumped, laughing as her elevated pulse found its natural equilibrium once more.

'The dark provides such easy terrors, do you not think?'

'All the easier when they have so captive an audience,' Percy teased.

'You may make fun of me, but I am sure you have your own.'

'I find no terror in the natural world, in neither darkness nor light. My terrors truly are my own, springing chiefly from my own inadequacies.'

Inadequacies, failures — these were not the words of passion. Mary wondered if now the moment of their physical union had come, he was preparing her for disappointment. Ridiculous, as she had nothing and no one to compare against.

'I worry I am not enough for you, Mary. You who command nature, whose birth shoots forth stars and comets that I can only celebrate in words. You are more than this earth; you are everything.'

'You are letting your imagination run away with you. The comet was not mine; it did not herald my arrival. It was a coincidence, nothing more. My life has been littered by coincidences, but seeing you again, being at the house when you came to visit — that has been the greatest moment of my life.'

Mary's nostrils filled with the sweet jasmine that perfumed the air; it was made all the sweeter by Percy's embrace. Her heart thumped loudly with the absolute surety of love.

'Let us go to our chamber, and share our poetry and passions.'

Mary took his hand, leading him wordlessly back through the moonlit garden and into the hotel. The weight of expectation pulled at her heart. She swallowed, hoping that Percy would not notice the tremble of her hand or the trepidation on her face. Having heard his laments and fears of disappointment, she was now besieged by fears of her own inexperience, praying that this false veneer of confidence would be enough.

Mary awoke to the guttering candle casting uncertain shadows around the room. Her hair was splayed out on the pillow in rivulets of untamed curls, the chill on her chest jolting her into sudden remembrance of her nudity. Percy, clad in an untied nightshirt, watched her as she brought herself back into consciousness, stretching one arm at a time.

'Are you well? How do you feel?' he asked.

Mary's body writhed in response, her slender frame transforming itself into this new shape of womanhood. She hardly recognised its movements. It would have come as no shock to her to open her mouth to speak, only to roar instead.

'I feel fearless!'

CHAPTER SIX

'I had always thought black to be a cooling colour, but then we do not see such persistent sunshine in London.' Mary pulled at the neck of her mourning dress, worn as a customary sign of respect to the grand French church. The vast interior of Notre Dame Cathedral was still warm, despite the thick stone walls and deep shadows.

'I feel terribly dull in these clothes.' Jane pushed the sides of her hair up, trying to elevate it to the same sculpted height as the coiffures of the fashionable French women who dominated the boulevards.

What Mary had seen of Paris so far bore little similarity to the Paris of her mother's descriptions. For one, it lacked the revolutionary zeal that infused her mother's journals. Instead of a proud city, shouting its victories with straight-backed flags and proclamations from every joyous tavern, she found a city defeated, one that wore its battles like fresh scabs. Even the countryside looked mournful, the gardens at the Tuileries composed of trees that bowed their heads self-consciously at those who walked past, and sad, half-grown blooms. It was impossible to tell whether they'd been cut off in their prime or had simply abandoned all hope of maturation. The locals turned their faces away from them, unwilling to accept anyone who had not suffered their struggles. Was it embarrassment or arrogance, Mary wondered? Either way, it was understandable that recent battles would give them scant incentive to be cordial.

Percy was unusually quiet, retreating into one of his long silences, which Mary was interpreting as a clear sign that something was troubling him. Their first night together had turned into a delicious haze of days lost in each other's arms, with scarcely any desire to go anywhere or do anything at all. Looking at him now and seeing a distracted glaze to his expression, she felt the separation more keenly.

Even the trip to the cathedral could not rouse his spirits, and the combination of his ill temper, the apathy of the locals, and the angry heat of the sun made it hard for Mary to keep her own good humour. Percy picked fault with every aspect of the cathedral's architecture and history — lamenting the gothic features felled by the conflicts, and pouring scorn on those recently added by Napoleon to add to the cathedral's bearing.

'Here, and here, there would have been ironwork ... magnificent ironwork housing the choir. There is no *authenticity* here!'

Percy stepped towards the altar, looking up at the figure of Christ upon the cross. In London, he had declared himself an atheist. In Wales, his views on religion had almost cost him his life. Now, Percy waved a hand dismissively, striding away from the altar. 'Why is beauty not cherished, Mary? Why is it not revered? Why?'

His voice echoed up to the ceiling, and around the colourful stained-glass windows where saints looked down at him with bemused expressions.

'I feel sure that even God himself would struggle to recognise this place from its picture,' Jane said as she walked towards them.

A local peasant woman praying in the front pew muttered as her hands crossed the air in front of her and then pushed past Percy. He wiped his brow, shook his head, and then he too stormed out of the cathedral.

'What's wrong with Percy today?' Jane asked. 'He is most definitely out of humour.'

'I do not know.' Mary shook her head. 'But I will learn. Stay here awhile. I will come and get you when the clouds have lifted.'

Mary found Percy sitting on a bench in front of some old graves that sat unevenly, like rows of crooked teeth. Only fragments of names and dates survived, the cherubs that remained upright having sacrificed wings or limbs to the elements. Percy's natural wildness looked at home in this setting. She breathed deeply, wanting to be sympathetic, but her forehead was sticky with sweat. Whoever said it was impossible to be in ill humour in the sunshine had never seen an Englishwoman without a hat in the midday sun.

'Is Notre Dame not pleasing to you?' She sat down on the bench next to him.

Percy shook his head. 'Perhaps I had overestimated its beauty, or underestimated the ravages against it. There are many things I find I am ill-prepared for.'

'Such as?' she ventured. The cathedral bells rang out, each peal emphasising the silence between them.

Percy inhaled deeply before speaking. 'I am running short of funds, Mary. I had not realised that hotels in Paris require long engagements, and I fear my money will not stretch as far as I'd hoped.'

'Can you not secure funds by some other means, a publisher perhaps?'

Percy snorted. 'No, there is no place for an English poet on French shelves. We are intruding upon them. They are grieving all they have lost. This is a time for consolidation, not innovation.'

'I have a ring, a necklace,' Mary said. 'I am sure they are not worth much, but they will be worth something. Take them and see if you can get any money.'

Percy shook his head. 'I have sold my gold pocket-watch and chain. What do you suppose I got for them?'

'Not their true value.' Mary fought back the tears that pricked at her eyes as she felt the shame of having swapped one precarious financial situation for another. She was ashamed of her lack of financial acumen and the stinging realisation of her absolute dependence on Percy and his family money. 'Twenty Napoleons?'

'Eight.' Percy slouched. 'I might as well have given it away.' He turned towards her, fresh grief etched on his features. 'I will see if I can secure some funds from a banker — if there are any fool enough to lend to me. My name, my title, might hold more sway here than it does in London.' He kissed her hand.

'The boulevards are clear and wide and the weather is on our side. We have no need of private coaches or expensive hotels, so long as we have each other.' Mary squeezed his hand.

'It was a lucky star that brought you to me, Mary.' He smiled. 'Now, let us retrieve poor Jane. She might have taken the habit during our absence.'

They walked back into the cathedral arm in arm. Though Percy's mood had lightened, Mary's stomach tightened at the thought of what being without money really meant: penury, poverty and — infinitely worse — the real possibility of having to go home.

They made their way back to Marais, the subsiding ferocity of the heat a welcome relief as they walked towards Parvis Notre-Dame. On the boulevards, the trees wore alternate coats of browns, reds and greens as if only distantly related, standing upright, still unconvinced they wouldn't be called upon to fight. One tree was hidden amongst the others, but its branches spread out with a wide confidence that encroached upon the space of all the others. *Brothers in arms or Napoleon, admitting defeat*, Mary thought as she walked past. A sudden gust of wind made the tree hiss in response. *Definitely Napoleon.*

There was something both majestic and unnerving about the houses that lined the pavements, their prominence proclaiming this to be a prosperous, desirable area. And yet the shutters on the windows, and the ivy that stretched out as if trying to make an escape, told a different story, a truer one. Men dressed from head to toe in black scurried from place to place, not opening a door without looking behind them. They populated the place now, the grand houses taken over by people who saw their move to Marais as a rise in social status. The air here, just like everywhere else they'd been in Paris, was heavy with sorrow and the drains below were stagnant with refuse.

'Jane,' said Percy, stopping, 'Mary and I have spoken, and I have a proposal for you.'

'A proposal?' She dropped the handkerchief she had been using to shield herself from the smells in surprise. 'What in the world can it be?'

'An adventure!' Percy's eyes shone.

Jane clasped her hands together. 'An adventure?' she gasped. Mary tried hard not to smirk, knowing that it was not the type of adventure Jane was expecting.

'We shall find a companion for our travels…'

'Yes!' Jane shot a look at Mary that screamed of superiority. Mary bit her lip to stop herself from laughing.

CHAPTER SEVEN

'A donkey … we went all that way for a donkey.' Jane scowled as she, Percy and the donkey approached Mary in the hotel garden.

'Not just any old donkey. Meet Napoleon.' Percy introduced him to Mary.

Mary stroked the donkey's cheek. 'I think he is very handsome.'

'Napoleon will be a grand accomplice for our journey; he can carry our luggage whilst we walk alongside.' Percy rubbed his hands together. 'Much cheaper than a coach too!'

Mary had spent an enjoyable day lounging about in the bedroom, reading poetry, while Percy and Jane braved the farms and markets in search of the donkey. Now the donkey was here, it could share the burden of their luggage or even themselves, should the journey prove too taxing.

'I am going to freshen up. I smell of horse manure and cow muck.' Jane's expression was thunderous.

'All very natural smells,' Percy said with a laugh. Jane strode away, her head high and her lips pursed. Mary could see that the adventure they had promised had not lived up to her expectations.

'Funds are very low, Mary,' Percy went on when they were alone. 'Buying Napoleon has depleted them further. Tomorrow, I must take myself to the bankers and see if any will advance money in my name.'

'Is it likely?'

'It has been heard of.'

'I have never seen you barter, and I would enjoy the time alone with you. Jane can spend the day with Napoleon.'

The next morning, they set off for the business district of Paris, passing through the Rue de Rivoli and Rue de Rohan. All the buildings looked the same — cast in limestone uniformity — and it seemed to Mary that they had trudged up and down the same roads countless times in their fruitless endeavour. She was tired, thirsty and wishing she had stayed at the hotel with the donkey. Percy knocked on every door, but few of them opened and those that did could not point him toward a banker who might help. Instead, they had bothered a number of merchants and the news of their endeavour must have been carried on the air, because by the time they reached the last door in the district, no one answered.

Percy slumped to the floor. Mary followed him. A well-dressed couple hurried past, throwing a gold coin at their feet. Percy scooped it up, his mouth open with horror as he prepared to get up.

'Monsieur, Madam…' he started.

Mary touched his arm and shook her head. 'Keep it. We might need it. At least we know that if all else fails, we can rely on *some* sympathy from the locals.'

'It won't get us very far, but it will get us some wine. Come on…'

Mary stood and dusted the limestone from her skirts. It would be a different proposition if they had letters of introduction or contacts they could seek. If Percy had secured publication in France and attained the success that was his destiny, then that too might have changed their circumstances. Mary wondered if fate was sending them signs that they shouldn't have been so impulsive — first Mary Jane arriving at the hotel in Calais before them, on the very packet steamer they'd rejected because it was too slow, and now this. No — this was a sign that they should have been more frugal and less extravagant in their earlier tastes. Taking rooms at the most popular hotel in Calais had been a misstep, one that had led them straight into Mary Jane's path. Had they not sought the most popular hotel, they would have held on to some money and some anonymity.

They had strayed off the main avenues and found themselves in a tucked-away part of the city, as far removed from the rigid restraints of the Rue d'Anjou as it was possible to imagine. The buildings huddled together as if whispering conspiratorially to each other. It was impossible to tell whether it was day or night here — time rolled together in corridors hewn in perpetual darkness, with only hints of artificial light. Opening a door to a smoky tavern, reluctant flames teetered nervously on tables full of men and serving women. All eyes turned towards Mary, who held on tightly to Percy's arm. Mutual horror froze them to the spot.

'Don't just stand there. You're blowing out the candles,' a server grunted.

Weaving a path through the drinkers and the smoke-filled air, they were relieved to find an empty table and sat themselves there. Wine was ordered, delivered and paid for, and once the novelty of their appearance had abated, they settled into a conversation that flowed as easily as the wine.

'What are we to do if we cannot secure any more funds?' Mary whispered to Percy, aware that the woman who had served their drinks was loitering near their table, rubbing the tables with a dirty cloth that had seen neither clean water nor beeswax in a long time, if ever.

'There must be other bankers in Paris. Failing that, I will endeavour to get a letter of introduction from … someone…' Percy waved a hand in the air dismissively.

'Is there no way of publishing *Queen Mab*? It would lend itself beautifully to translation.'

'It would, but I'm still paying for the English print.' He hesitated, gazing into his drink mournfully. 'And it hardly set the world alight.'

'Perhaps not, but if your sleeve fans any closer to the candle, that might.'

'Oh, bother…' Percy flapped his sleeve in the air. Mary laughed. The eyes of the tavern turned back to them momentarily.

That broke the tension and Percy clasped Mary's hand, kissing it enthusiastically.

'What would I do without you, Mary? You can chase away even the darkest of shadows.'

The woman who had been watching them slid away, moving back behind the bar, where she spoke to a ruddy-cheeked man whose bearing reminded Mary of a walrus she had seen in one of her father's books. He eyed them with the same suspicion as the woman, nodded his head, then turned away. Percy fell back into a sigh, oblivious to their stare, but Mary's curiosity was piqued and she followed their movements behind the bar, feeling sure that some attempt at conversation would follow. Sure enough, moments later, the man came over to their table with a second carafe of wine.

'No, sir, we have not ordered more wine.' Percy waved the wine away.

'You are English?' the man asked. Up close, a small sandy-coloured moustache peppered his lip.

Percy and Mary nodded.

'And you are looking to make money, I hear?'

Percy's eyes darted towards the bar; the woman had disappeared.

'I do not appreciate private conversations being the subject of tavern tittle-tattle...' Percy shuffled in his seat.

Mary put her hand on his arm. 'Let us not be too hasty, Percy. We do not yet know what is on offer. Is this for us?' She gestured towards the wine. The walrus man nodded and took the stopper out. Percy gulped his remaining wine down, pushing his glass forward for a re-fill.

'I have a patron — a banker — who is in a difficult situation, one which he cannot sort out himself.' The man shrugged. 'It is a sensitive matter that requires ... discretion.'

'Is it a police matter?' Mary asked.

'He prefers to keep it away from Le Gendarmerie for as long as he can.'

'Then it is something unsavoury and not the sort of thing we care to become involved in,' Percy said with a sniff.

Mary smiled. For a liberal thinker, Percy could be staggeringly conventional when it suited him. Perhaps this might be just the sort of distraction he needed; in fact, a meeting with this banker might even ease their financial woes. To her mind, they could not afford to dismiss this chance.

'Do you have a calling card for your friend?' she asked, catching Percy's eye as he shook his head at her in disbelief. It was good to know she could still surprise him.

Clutching the card for one Monsieur Lamont, Mary felt braver and more confident as they made their way back through the dark passageways of Paris, out from the underbelly that the city turned its gaze away from. She was sure that she could land a good kick, punch or swing of her bag if it came to it. At least there were no valuables on her person, no outward displays of wealth that might shine a spotlight on them, even in these shadowy recesses. Besides, the wine and talk of enigmatic bankers with unspecified problems had invigorated her spirit, making her mind race through the possibilities of his problem.

'What do you think has happened?' she asked Percy, relaxing as they turned back towards more familiar boulevards.

'I do not know; it could be anything or nothing. One man's "difficult situation" may be nothing more than a trifle to another.'

Mary grinned, glad that the dusky sky obscured it. An irrepressible theatricality often accompanied Percy's bouts of terror or spontaneity; he would be well placed on the stages of the theatres they strolled past. Mary was only just learning to distinguish genuine emergencies from his imagined ones. Unfortunately, the lack of money was a real problem, but perhaps a visit to this Monsieur Lamont would provide a swift remedy.

Monsieur Lamont's office crouched in a passageway under the arch at the junction between Rue d'Anjou and Rue Nationale. Studs in the shape of a cross pierced its glossy wooden door, distinguishing it from the other blank doorways. The door creaked open, revealing an elderly man with curved shoulders and white hair. He scrutinised them through thick-lensed spectacles.

'Monsieur Lamont?' Percy repeated until a spark of recognition appeared in the old man's face.

'Up there.' The man pointed a shaking finger up the stairs, before retreating into the building. For an elderly man, he moved quickly and lightly. Together, Percy and Mary climbed the staircase, Mary's skirt rustling against the stone steps like dry autumn leaves. At the top was another door.

Percy knocked on the door and turned the handle. 'Monsieur Lamont?'

They found Monsieur Lamont sitting behind an enormous desk in front of a small window which let in little light. He looked up at his name and beckoned them in.

'Yes, how may I help you?'

'Please excuse the intrusion without introduction. Your name was given to us. I believe you have a delicate task you need help with.'

Lamont stared at them, then gestured for them to sit down in the two chairs opposite him, offering nothing more in the way of pleasantries or greetings. His mouth was a thin, straight line.

'And who told you that, may I ask?' He steepled his fingers in front of him and looked between Percy and Mary.

'A man in a tavern.' Mary coughed, heat rising to her cheeks at the impropriety of a respectable woman visiting a tavern. It was unheard of in London.

If Lamont thought it improper, however, he said nothing. Instead, he asked, 'How much do you know about my situation?'

'Nothing, except that it is a delicate matter and demands discretion.'

'And how do I know you can offer discretion? Is it because you are English?'

'We are writers and philosophers, thinkers and theorists. We are a good many things that do not define us. I fear we have wasted your time and ours. Good day to you.' Percy stood up to leave. Mary glared at him, shaking her head. Contrite, he sat down again.

'We need money, and you have a task you will pay for. To me, that sounds like the basis for a sound negotiation,' she said, smiling.

'My wife has gone missing.' Monsieur Lamont spoke slowly. 'I want you to find her. It is as simple and as difficult as that.'

'I am sorry to hear that. Do you have any idea where she may have gone?'

'Yes, many, but I am a busy man, and I cannot afford the time away from my business.'

'Your business is more important to you than her welfare?' Mary asked, surprised.

'Of course not,' Lamont snapped. 'But I fear she does not wish to be found by me, if it is something that I have done, or something that she has done, which has caused her to leave. Either way, I don't care.' He sank back in his chair. 'I just want her to be found.'

'Very well.' Mary straightened her shoulders. 'And what is to be the reward?'

'I can pay only fifty francs.'

'Fifty?' Mary spluttered, hardly able to contain her astonishment at the vast sum.

'Sixty then,' said Lamont, misinterpreting her response. 'I will go no higher than that. Thirty now and thirty on completion of the task.'

Percy looked at Mary. She shuffled in her seat, scarcely able to hide her excitement.

'All right, let's get straight to business.' Mary rubbed her hands together. 'Tell us everything we need to know.'

CHAPTER EIGHT

Mary took out a quill and a sheet of paper while Percy paced around the hotel room, the soft bray of the donkey carried on the evening breeze through the open window. Percy spoke as he walked.

'Claudine Lamont was expected at the Théâtre Montansier at eight o'clock on the Wednesday night, but never arrived. Monsieur Lamont had been on business in Troyes and was on his way back to meet her there. He returned home but she was not there and, as far as he knows, none of his wife's possessions are missing. Their house is near to the theatre and has a few servants, all of whom claim to know nothing about Madame Lamont's disappearance almost three weeks ago.'

'Correct,' Mary replied. 'Though you miss one point. The staff are unlikely to share their suspicions with Monsieur Lamont, however benevolent he is. We will go the house tomorrow and interview the staff.'

'And what, exactly, are we to ask them?'

'Well, we know what time Madame Lamont was expected at the theatre, and we know that she never arrived, so we can ask what they know about her last known movements — how she was dressed, when she left the house, if she even left the house at all.'

'Excellent, Mary, yes!' Percy shot a triumphant fist into the air; it was a gesture that usually signified that he was happy with a piece of imagery or a couplet. 'What else?'

'Then we shall make enquires of her friends and acquaintances — where she goes, who she sees. We shall try to paint a picture of the lady and her habits.'

'Right, right.' Percy sat down on the edge of the bed. 'What is your first instinct for this, Mary? You seem to have a better nose for this than I do.'

'You are a poet — you see things how they *should* be, not always as they are. Women are infinitely more practical, don't you think?'

Percy frowned. Mary could see he was trying to decide how to take her comments. In the end, he seemed to opt for taking them in good humour, which was a great relief.

'All this detection is making me quite hungry,' he said, standing again. 'Shall we see how Jane and Napoleon have spent the day?'

Château Lamont was vast, hidden behind rows of poplars, its very seclusion making it stand out — as if attempting to hide its wealth and grandeur only amplified it. The house was cast in the same limestone as Monsieur Lamont's businesses — another signifier of fortune — and Mary tried to tidy her hair and pinch some colour into her cheeks as they made their way up the path towards the front door. A woman at the window watched them, but bid a hasty retreat into the house as Mary waved to her. Perhaps she thought they were merchants or maybe even criminals.

Mary's black dress crunched with every step; it really was time to get their clothes cleaned. Why hadn't she thought of these things when they'd planned the elopement? It was fine being swept away with the romance of escape, but when your clothes smelt like a sweaty ocean, it wasn't conducive to romance. Sadly, there were no instructions on such matters in the travel journals of her mother, nor in any of Byron's poetry.

They gathered at the door like a motley choir. Napoleon screeched. Mary did not know why they had brought

Napoleon along with them — that was Percy's idea — and Jane looked less than thrilled. Monsieur Lamont's missing wife had fired something in Mary's imagination, and she was determined to take on an active role in finding her — this was just the sort of distraction she needed from the perpetual travel sickness that had plagued her since the start of their journey. Mary could not believe that they had only been away from Somers Town for a month. She felt like she had aged twenty years in that time and wondered if she would even recognise the young woman she had left behind — or if her father or Fanny would recognise her now. Thoughts of her father pained her. He had not replied to her letters nor made any effort of his own to get in touch with her. It stung to think of him back in London, listening to Harriet's scurrilous attack on her integrity, but she knew him well enough to know that any attempt to cajole him into a desired response would generate the opposite one.

The creaking of the door snapped Mary out of her thoughts. Napoleon brayed a greeting before any of them had a chance to offer theirs. Mary was surprised that the door was opened by a young woman in a maid's uniform, not much older than herself, and not the woman she had seen from the window. She gave what she hoped was a warm and friendly smile. It was returned with a shy bow of the head.

'We have been hired by Monsieur Lamont to discover the whereabouts of Madame Lamont,' Mary said. 'Could we come in and ask some questions?'

'Does Monsieur think we have anything to do with Madam's disappearance?' the young woman asked with a gulp.

'No. He does not know what has happened. He is just keen to find her.'

That reassured the young woman, who opened the door wide and invited them in.

'You can leave your donkey over there, out of the sun.' She pointed to a sheltered spot with a gate and a tree canopying the area. Napoleon trotted over reluctantly, but he was soon compensated with a bowl of water and a couple of carrots. Mary's stomach grumbled; she remembered that she'd forgotten to partake of breakfast that morning, she had been so keen to get here. She was regretting it now and had half a mind to steal one of Napoleon's carrots.

'Please, come in. I know high tea is customary in England, but would you care for coffee?'

'Yes, please,' Mary answered quickly, hoping the coffee would settle her stomach. Neither Mary nor Jane had tried coffee until they had come to France; they both felt very grown up and cosmopolitan whenever they drank it. Percy, of course, was better versed in continental ways than they were.

'We will need to speak to all the staff,' Percy said once they were settled in the morning room. 'We have Monsieur Lamont's authorisation to do so.'

'The cook has gone to market, so it is only me and Patrice, the gardener, here at the moment.'

'When are you expecting the cook back?'

'Not until this afternoon. When Madame is here, there is lunch to prepare, but as she is not here and Monsieur prefers to stay at work, there is no call for lunch to be prepared. Unless, of course, you would like some?'

Although Mary's stomach rumbled at the mention of the word, they were here to undertake a job that they'd already been paid handsomely for.

'Thank you, but no, coffee will be more than sufficient,' Mary answered.

Jane's and Percy's shoulders sagged with disappointment.

Mary looked around the room while the maid went to prepare the coffee. The ceiling was high, the walls panelled in white and painted above in the faintest duck-egg blue. An ornate candelabra added to the decadent display. The clink of fine china announced the maid's return. Once she'd placed the tray in front of them and poured out their drinks, she shifted uncomfortably. Sitting in this room was something she clearly was unused to.

'Please, take a seat,' said Percy, indicating an armchair. 'Tell us about yourself.'

The maid perched on the edge. 'My name is Marie, I am eighteen years old, and I have worked for the Lamont family for two years.' She nodded, folding her hands in front of her.

Mary smiled reassuringly at Marie. 'Can you tell us about Madame Lamont? Is she a good employer?'

'As the Lamonts are my first employers, I have nothing to compare them to. They have always been clear in my duties and fair in my treatment.' Marie shrugged. 'I have no complaints.'

'Would you say that you are friendly with Madame Lamont?'

Marie hesitated before replying. 'No, I would not say friendly. I know my duties and I execute them to the best of my ability. I do not seek nor expect friendship.'

'How is the relationship between Monsieur and Madame Lamont?' Jane cut in. Mary frowned at her.

'I would say it is the same as the relationship between any other husband and wife in Paris. No better. No worse. It appears to be strong, but what do I know of love? Who am I to judge?'

'Can you think of any reason for Madame Lamont's disappearance?' Mary asked, delving deeper now Jane had opened the door.

'None.' Marie rose from her seat. 'If there is nothing else, perhaps I can continue with my duties?'

'Can you show us to Madame Lamont's rooms?' Mary asked, also rising to her feet.

They walked out of the room and Mary continued to ask polite questions of the maid, as if making casual conversation. This informal mode of questioning suited Marie better, and by the time they reached Madame Lamont's rooms, Mary had learnt of Madame's daily routine — letter-writing in the morning, a walk in the afternoon, accepting calls from friends — and of her great friendship with Madame Thibeaux.

Mary and Percy thanked Marie as she turned and walked back downstairs. Claudine Lamont's rooms were a series of connected chambers that walked her through each stage of her daily preparations. A simple bathroom contained the sort of bath that Cleopatra would have bathed in; the dressing room to its side housed a grand table with a large, gilded mirror whose cherubs smiled back at Mary as she looked in it. But it was the bedroom that took her breath away, bathed in a golden light that filtered through the lace curtains of the opulent four-poster bed.

'Can we stay here, please?' Jane put a hand to her head as if the rooms were too beautiful for her to bear, then she exclaimed, 'Mary, look at these!'

Mary turned away from the bed and looked at the open wardrobe, bursting with fine silk dresses in all the colours of the rainbow. Hues of purple, gold and green shone with a religious fervour against the deep mahogany of the wooden backdrop. Jane ran a hand across the dresses.

'Can you imagine the jewels that accompany these dresses?' She was practically swooning.

Mary scanned the room again, making an inventory of the wide windows, wardrobe, bed and bedside table. There were certainly enough displays of wealth, but very little sign of anything personal. There were no books, no ornaments, not even a desk or bureau in which to find secret journals or half-written letters.

'There is no key for the lock...' Percy pulled at the drawer of the bedside table. 'I have a capital way of opening it — do you think I should?'

'I do not know, Percy.' An uneasy feeling settled in Mary's stomach. Being in Madame Lamont's private space, going through her possessions, felt intrusive.

As if reading her thoughts, Percy put an arm around Mary. 'We have been paid to find Madame Lamont, and we cannot do that unless we learn more about her.'

Mary sighed and nodded. 'Open it, but do not leave it in such a state that our intrusion is obvious.'

Percy rubbed his hands together, extracted the penknife he used for sharpening quills, and knelt by the bedside table. Moments later the drawer sprang out.

'Huzzah!' Percy exclaimed.

Mary carefully extracted the neat assembly of invitations, play bills and a book from the drawer, spreading them out on the bed.

'Look for names, addresses, anything that might be of note.'

Jane had pried herself away from the dresses and sprang towards the book.

'It is the latest Lord Byron collection; I wonder if I could borrow it.'

Mary took the book from her hands and opened it, revealing the portrait of Byron that adorned the title page. Percy's eyes went to the book, and a sigh of admiration passed over his lips.

'One day, this will be you,' Mary soothed. She closed the book. 'Anything else of note — aside from her love of poetry?'

'An invitation to an exhibition…' Jane rifled through the invitations. 'A ticket to the opera, a ticket to a charity ball held by Madame Thibeaux… It has her address, look.'

Jane passed the invitation to Mary. She made a mental note of the address and charity. The sum of Claudine Lamont's personal possessions showed that until now, her life had been the very model of respectability. She had been seen in the right places and supported the worthiest of causes, but also had her finger on the pulse of popular literature.

'I think we have uncovered all that we will learn here. Next, we must speak to the gardener.' Mary placed the items back in the drawer with meticulous care.

As they made their way back through the labyrinth of corridors, Mary began to think that they had got lost. The way up had been so direct, she could not understand why it was proving difficult to find their way back down.

'I do not remember passing this room before…' Jane pointed to an open door. A giant portrait of a man in hunting attire stared back at them with a formidable expression. 'What room do you suppose that to be?'

'If it is an upstairs chamber, then it must be a bedroom or a guest room,' Mary reasoned.

Jane grimaced. 'Well, I could not sleep with that monstrous face gazing down at me. I should have nothing but nightmares.'

'It draws me in…' Percy strode past them, straight into the bedroom. 'Come on.' He beckoned them inside.

The room that greeted them was as cluttered and busy as Madame Lamont's was neat and tidy; paperwork spilt from every surface, concealing the furniture beneath. Newspapers, letters and bills were strewn everywhere, as if it had not long before been ransacked by a burglar.

'This surely cannot be Monsieur Lamont's chamber? Can it?' Mary asked, recalling the efficiency of his business chambers.

'It is as if his every thought, hobby or habit is laid out on each surface.' Percy shook his head.

Mary and Jane exchanged a knowing look. Percy covered every table, wall, floor and even the windows with his poems and scribbles. If Mary closed her eyes, she could picture his lodgings, in which daylight was obliterated by works in progress. It was only a matter of time before their hotel room was similarly decorated.

'I am surprised he can find anything in here,' she said.

'I am sure there is a brilliant method to his system,' Jane countered. 'However, if anything is lost, I am sure he could ask his companion for help.' She looked up at the giant portrait and shivered.

'Come on, let us away.' Mary ushered them out of the room, closing the door behind them. The staircase was right in front of them. Mary frowned. Had it been there the whole time? If there was one consolation of living in a smaller house, it was that one never feared getting lost. They walked down the stairs and out of the door. The gardener was pruning a hedge near where Napoleon was grazing.

Percy put his hand on Mary's shoulder. 'I will lay the groundwork here,' he said, and coughed to attract the gardener's attention.

It took several more coughs before the man cast a glance in their direction. 'What is it?' he asked gruffly, his eyes wrinkling against the sunlight.

'We are here to investigate the disappearance of Madame Lamont,' Percy started.

'Oh yes.' He snapped at the topiary with his shears.

'You seem to have missed a bit, there.' Percy pointed to a section of the hedge where a solitary strand stood out stubbornly. The gardener looked at Percy, before grunting and snapping inches away from Percy's finger. The errant piece fell to the ground.

'What do you want with me?' he asked. 'Not as though Madame had anything to do with the garden, except for having tea parties in the summer.' He sniffed; his voice was tinged with more than a hint of disdain.

'How long have you worked for Monsieur and Madame Lamont?' Mary asked, deciding that her line of questioning could not be any less satisfactory than Percy's.

'A year, two years, ever since I was discharged from the navy.'

'You were in the navy?' Percy interjected, all ears.

'I was, but that was a lifetime ago, and I'm a gardener now.' The tone of the gardener's voice informed them that that was as much as he was going to say on the subject. Percy looked a little dejected.

'It is a beautiful garden; it must be a lot of work,' said Mary.

'Yes, it is, but I'm not afraid of hard work, and I enjoy getting my hands dirty.'

'Do you live on site?'

'Used to. I have a small flat on the other side of Paris. The less desirable end.' His worn hands were a sharp contrast to

Percy's delicate fingers. No better demonstration of the differences between the classes had Mary ever seen.

'When did you last see Madame Lamont?'

'I hardly ever see her. Like I say, she only comes out here when she's having a party and she wants to make sure the garden's at its best. She likes the roses.' He turned away from them to continue his pruning.

It was clear to Mary that she wouldn't get any more from him, that if he had any opinion of Madame Lamont at all, it wasn't a high one. They were wasting their time here.

Jane untied the donkey, and they made their way back onto the boulevard.

'Well, that wasn't exactly productive, was it?' Jane said.

'We learnt that Madame Lamont wasn't the kind of woman to have a lot to do with her staff,' Mary countered.

'Shall we try to find the cook at the market?' Jane asked.

'Are you suggesting that because you think we will find her there? Or is it because you are hungry and want food?' Mary chided.

Defeated, Jane pulled at the donkey's rein, walking in front of Percy and Mary.

'I think she is feeling left out, Mary,' Percy said. 'Be kinder to her.'

Mary sighed. It was true; she and Percy had been so wrapped up in each other that they had hardly given Jane a second thought. Perhaps it was time that Mary remembered the kindness Jane had shown them, all the letters she had secreted to and from one another when they were planning their elopement, how discreet she had been. She would be kinder.

'As you wish, Jane!' Mary called.

Jane turned around. 'Pardon?'

'Let us go to the market and see if we can learn anything there.'

All they learnt was that the market stalls were sparse, save for hard cheeses and stale bread, which was quickly becoming their regular cuisine. Apart from livestock and the occasional stall selling items that looked to have been looted from grand houses, the markets were depressing and did little to assuage their hunger. At least they had stopped to eat, and Napoleon seemed glad of a round of hay, carrots and water.

The afternoon was milder than its predecessors, so they traced the route back from the Château Lamont to the Théâtre Montansier at which Madame Lamont never arrived. Unlike the back streets Mary and Percy got lost in previously, these streets were wide and open, with no passages or alleys that offered the opportunity to take a person off their intended course.

'Perhaps we should visit the theatre while we are here?' Mary suggested. 'There are some comedies and Shakespeare this season.'

'Is it *Hamlet*?' Jane asked, eyes wide with renewed enthusiasm. 'France is a bit like Hamlet now, haunted by the ghost of its past.'

'That is a deep thing to say when you're standing next to a donkey,' Percy said with a chuckle.

'Napoleon here is a born philosopher,' Jane stated defiantly.

A twinge of jealousy stabbed at Mary's heart as laughter flowed between them. Percy and Jane's relationship was simple and uninhibited. Whatever she had with Percy, it was not that.

'What were they going to watch?' Mary asked suddenly.

'What?' Percy replied.

'At the theatre, what was the show they were going to see? Did Monsieur Lamont say?'

'No.' Percy shook his head. 'I don't think he did.'

'We need to get a journal,' Mary added. 'We must write down all of our questions in case we forget them.'

'How often are we to report to Monsieur Lamont?' Percy asked.

'He didn't specify.' Mary bit her lip. 'But we will need to ask him more questions once we know what our next steps should be.'

For now, their next steps were back to the hotel for a couple of hours of reading and relaxing. Spending all their time thinking about Monsieur Lamont's missing wife would do nothing to restore their imaginations or fire their inquisitive natures. Detection, like anything else, needed to be nurtured and respected, but it also needed time for each small clue to burst to life, to grow roots and show its full bloom. Mary needed something taxing to fool her mind into a different kind of mental release. She knew exactly what she must do — she must practise her Greek verbs.

CHAPTER NINE

Mary's sleep was uneasy and fitful, her mind plagued by the nightmare that had haunted her since her childhood. It was the same dream she'd always had. She is a child again, running along a sandy beach where all seems beautiful and calm until a sudden darkness descends, and she finds herself in a strange, cavernous place only partially known — a cave or some other dark place visited on a family trip. Darkness invades her senses like a fog, choking her from the inside. She watches as the fog takes on a monstrous human shape and a twisting sensation at her neck becomes the grip of long, finely carved fingers, seemingly chiselled out of bone. The rest of the body comes into focus bit by bit: the hand attached to a sinewy arm, the arm to a hollowed shoulder, the shoulder to a neck and then a head where dark shadows caress the spaces underneath the eyes —

'Mary? Mary, what is it?'

The sensation of being shaken awake shattered the vision and Mary stared up into Percy's fearful face. Her heart thudded, rendering all speech impossible as Percy rushed to light a candle. The flame dispelled the gloom, but it took longer to chase the shadows away.

'Percy…' She clasped at her throat. 'A drink. Have we any water?'

The hipflask was offered instead. Mary grabbed it and gulped the liquid down, the alcohol extinguishing her fear and replacing it with a warm sensation in her throat.

She'd first had the dream when her father had announced he meant to find a wife, and it subsequently returned when least expected. In the dream, the demon's grip had eventually loosened. As it walked away, another shadowy figure took its place. Mary recognised the stoic, upright gait and the worn dress coat. She knew exactly who it was. Her father.

'Are you well?' The candlelight illuminated the concern on Percy's face.

'I am now. It is nothing, Percy, just a night-terror. It is nothing to be concerned about.'

'But you screamed out. You thrashed about the bed, as if trying to grab an assailant.'

Mary gasped. Percy was holding his arm; a small line of red seeped through his nightshirt.

'Did I do that?' she stammered.

'It is nothing more than a scratch. You lashed out when I tried to wake you.'

'I am sorry, Percy. I should have warned you of this. Sometimes I dream I am being chased by a monstrous figure that seems almost human. It follows me because it is angry with me, because I have abandoned it. Ridiculous, isn't it?'

'Terrors are often the cornerstones of fantastic poems. Perhaps by turning it into verse you may expunge it?'

'I prefer your words to mine and need only your arms to console me.'

Mary pulled Percy close, the press of his body chasing the nightmare from her mind. Here she could happily obliterate all horrors, replace them with sweet kisses and even sweeter thoughts, but the darkness lingered, casting a shadow on the far wall, reminding her it was never far behind.

As a luxurious sunrise welcomed them into the new day, Mary awoke feeling refreshed and safe in Percy's arms. She lay there contemplating everything that had passed and the mission they found themselves on.

Where would they begin to look for an unknown person in an unknown city? Surely it was an impossible task. The little information they had gleaned from their conversations at the Château Lamont had furnished them with nothing more than a couple of names and a vague description of Madame Lamont, and gave no indication of why she would want to disappear, or why anyone else would wish for her disappearance. Mary's mind raced through possibilities — perhaps they could go back to the house and talk to the cook. She tapped her foot. Where was that journal they'd recently purchased? She needed to make a list.

Carefully lifting Percy's arm from her chest, Mary slid out of the bed and tiptoed over to the desk. Fragments of Percy's half-written poems dotted the table, with snail trails of black ink beside them. Mary picked up the quill, dipped it into the ink, and drew a piece of paper towards her. She tapped at her lips with the quill, retracing their steps in her mind, then wrote down all that was known and all that was unknown. Apart from the certainties of Madame Lamont's name, and where and when she was supposed to meet her husband, other facts were thin on the ground.

Remembering the map of Paris in Percy's pocket, Mary opened it out and ran her finger over the route from Château Lamont to the Théâtre Montansier. Madame Lamont could have been kidnapped; they were clearly a family with money. And yet the mood of the city was one of apathy and heartbreak, not greed and jealousy, and if she had been kidnapped by someone intending to extort money from Monsieur Lamont, surely there would have been some form of communication by now? No, that wasn't it. Judging by her charity work, Claudine Lamont was a benevolent employer;

surely if someone had come to her for help, she would have tried to help them.

There was nothing. It was as if Madame Lamont had simply disappeared from the face of the earth. To offer nothing, to give no word — could you do that to someone who loved you? Mary would not have believed it possible if it weren't for the silence that stretched between herself and her father. If he could disown her so easily, then perhaps it was she who was the odd one for caring too much.

Another possibility presented itself — perhaps Madame Lamont had vanished because she wanted to disappear. But why? Could she have been embroiled in a love-affair and left Paris in order to avoid a scandal? Mary's cheeks flushed as she thought of Harriet discarded by Percy, her stomach blooming while her marriage withered and died. Guilt twisted her own stomach into knots — it was no surprise that she had spent much of the journey feeling sick. If she thought about the repercussions of their actions, the effects on other people's lives, it was almost too much to bear. Love had made a monster of her. It was no wonder her own monster was chasing her through the landscape of her dreams. She had brought him here with her, as surely as if he'd had a ticket and boarded the coach with them. He was her constant and would remain so for the entirety of their journey. Perhaps Madame Lamont had monsters of her own.

Mary turned back to the map. It was high season, and almost the time in which Parisian socialites retire to the countryside to relax amongst the green tranquillity of their country homes, if they still had them. Perhaps Madame Lamont had gone to the countryside? She and her husband were clearly cultured people — the paintings, books and theatre tickets were testament to that. What had Marie told them of Claudine's rituals? Letters in the morning, a walk in the afternoon, accepting calls from friends — most of whom were the wives of Monsieur Lamont's business acquaintances.

Mary shuddered at the memory of the gardener, slicing the topiary with murderous intent. Patrice had a hardness of expression that troubled her. They had learnt nothing from him except Madame Lamont's love of roses. He did not share Marie's enthusiasm for their employers; but then, Mary couldn't imagine what it was — other than plants — that he might get enthusiastic about. Would it be worth going to see the cook? Would they learn anything from her? The likelihood of Claudine Lamont spilling her soul to someone stirring soups and pummelling bread was slim.

No, Mary needed to question Madame Lamont's friends and confidants — people who called her Claudine, who knew her secrets, who could give them a clue as to where she might have gone. She suddenly recalled the address of Madame Thibeaux, which she had memorised from the ticket to the charity ball, and jotted it down in the journal. Madame Thibeaux, Marie had told them, had been Madame Lamont's friend.

Mary, Percy, Jane and Napoleon made their way south from Marais to the sixth arrondissement. Passing through the different arrondissements in the early morning sun was like discovering all the different facets of Paris's personality — this was the artistic district and somewhere nearer to the Paris that Mary had been expecting. The streets were lively and loud, with accordion players braving the summer heat to bring mournful military marches and fanfares to the streets. Here, the women deviated away from the stacked hairstyles of the fashionably scornful centre and an atmosphere of hope, forgiveness and acceptance perfumed the air. *This is more like it,*

Mary thought to herself. Even Napoleon agreed, braying loudly as he was fed a carrot by the patron of the café they had stopped at.

They enjoyed a café au lait and pastries as they watched the world go by and gained their bearings. The patron had not batted an eyelid at the sight of Napoleon tethered to the arm of Percy's chair, while Mary almost began to regret tethering themselves to Lamont's task, wishing she could bask in the glow of this convivial atmosphere. Here was the sort of place that inspired poetry. Having whiled away an hour — they would happily have whiled away a day — Mary reluctantly asked the patron for directions to Madame Thibeaux's address.

'It is an apartment, two roads down,' he told her, wiping glasses with a cloth as he spoke. 'But there are stairs to it; you cannot take your donkey.'

Mary returned to the table. Jane and Napoleon had both turned their faces towards the sun, wearing twin expressions of joy and relaxation.

'I have the directions,' Mary said.

Jane opened one eye lazily in response. 'Is it far?'

'No, but it involves stairs, which will not be suitable for the donkey.'

'Then Napoleon and I shall stay here. I shall recite Molière's *Misanthrope* to him.' Jane reached into her bag, extracted her book and rested a hand upon it, closing the matter.

'Shall we go, Mary?' Percy asked, scattering francs like small gold suns on the table as they left.

Half an hour later they still hadn't found Madame Thibeaux's apartment, and Mary conceded the map was little help when faced with the maze of arrondissements not yet included on it. The sun, which had seemed so warm and relaxing when basking in the shade of the café, now bore down on them aggressively, exacerbating their agitation.

'Surely it must be around here somewhere?' said Mary, darting glances in all directions lest she should miss a valuable turning.

'Let us find someone to ask,' Percy suggested, stopping to talk to a man who scuttled along the pavement like a busy beetle. While Mary continued to scrutinise the street names, Percy's voice was an exasperated breeze in the distance.

'Over here.' He beckoned her over, his other hand pointing in the opposite direction. 'He says it is over here.'

Sure enough, the road sign confirmed that they had come to the right place. Mary wiped her brow, put the map back in her bag, and prepared herself.

'Perhaps you should knock,' said Percy. 'A lady is unlikely to answer the door to a strange gentleman.'

'That all depends on how strange the gentleman is … or how handsome.' Mary smiled at him as she took the large brass knocker in her hand and rapped it upon the wood. A muffled voice and the sound of footsteps confirmed that somebody was at home, and a moment later the door opened with a slow curiosity. Behind it stood a very short, elderly woman in a black dress and with a fashionably high hairstyle.

'*Oui?*' she asked.

Mary explained who they were and why they were there. The old woman listened attentively, nodded, then ushered them inside and up the staircase to the apartment.

'Madame?' The small woman's voice bellowed into the hallway, the reverberation making her temperamental hair shake.

They were ushered into a plush sitting room with a large window, in which Paris was framed like a panoramic painting.

A large golden chair was placed next to a birdcage of the same hue, from which a colourful parrot watched them.

'Please take a seat. Don't mind Monsieur Francis; he is quiet around strangers.'

Madame Thibeaux, when she appeared, was a sprightly woman in her seventies with patrician features and a similarly perilous hairstyle to her maid.

'Tea?' she asked. 'I have it imported. The very finest.'

Madame Thibeaux called to the maid, who appeared and disappeared in black-shrouded silence, reappearing with a tea set that reflected golden versions of themselves back at them.

'I know it is not the hour for cake, but I cannot be social without it and Monsieur Francis will pay less heed to our conversation if he eats.'

The word cake made Mary's stomach gurgle in delight; they had become used to practically scavenging for milk, bread and cheese in a land which had little to spare.

'That would be splendid,' Percy answered, saving Mary the effort.

Tea and cake were served and enjoyed, and Madame Thibeaux wiped a stray crumb from her lip before turning back to the conversation.

'How can I help you?' she asked. Her advanced age clearly had done nothing to diminish her senses or her ability to cut to the chase.

'You are friends with Claudine Lamont? We have been hired by her husband to investigate her disappearance,' Mary replied, just as directly.

'*Detectus*, meaning to uncover or expose … and what do you expect to expose?' She leant forward, her eyes meeting Mary's with a mischievous twinkle. Mary could see why Madame Lamont would befriend her.

'That is entirely the point — we do not know.'

'It is very easy for women to disappear in Paris; it happens all the time. I myself have disappeared many times over the years; each time is a reinvention.'

'Do you think that is what Madame Lamont has done? Chosen to disappear?'

Madame Thibeaux looked to the parrot cage before answering. 'Claudine is a free spirit, trapped in a gilded cage. It would not surprise me at all if she *has* opened the door and flown away.' She stood up and pointed at the cage. 'May I?' Mary and Percy nodded, and she opened the cage door. Everyone waited to see if, given the chance of freedom, the parrot would take it. He didn't.

'Though we may dream of freedom, only the brave accept it,' Madame Thibeaux concluded.

'And was she?' Mary asked. 'Brave, I mean?'

The elderly lady stroked the parrot through the cage, trying to coax him onto her arm.

'No, I would not say that she was brave, but I would not say that she was unhappy, either. Sometimes we sit in our cage for so long that we no longer notice the bars.'

Mary looked at Percy. His eyes were wide with the same look of admiration he had whenever her father started talking.

'Could you perhaps tell us more about her?'

The parrot settled on her shoulder, and Madame Thibeaux slowly sat back down in her chair.

'Claudine and I have been friends for years. My late husband worked with Pierre Lamont, and we used to go to the theatre together, take trips to the countryside. When my husband passed, our friendship continued, but I do not get out as much as I used to, so our meetings have been largely conducted here

… under Monsieur Francis's watchful eye.' She tipped her head to the parrot, who squawked in response.

'Does Madame Lamont have any other friends? Or perhaps enemies? Anyone who would wish her harm?'

Madame Thibeaux pursed her lips and shook her head. 'No, Claudine is a shy, kind woman. She is not the sort to confront or be confronted. She enjoys simple pleasures and lives simply. She cares not for exhibitions of wealth; she enjoys painting, reading, flowers. She likes to help people. A very beautiful lady, a very typical French lady. Here.'

Madame Thibeaux dived into her pocket and extracted a small, oval portrait locket that she held in her palm like a bird, allowing only the gold rim of the top to be visible. Mary watched her knuckles whiten around it as she weighed up her next steps.

'Is Madame Lamont a very beautiful person?'

'She is possessed of great inner and outer beauty. She is intoxicating — which makes her disappearance all the more extraordinary.' Madame Thibeaux sighed, tightening her grip on the locket until the veins protruded in her hand. Mary's heart quickened; she needed that likeness.

'I have been trying to picture her; Monsieur Lamont gave scant details of her physical appearance and there were no personal objects in his office. He is a brusque man, officious both in shape and stature. But she is different — to me, she is soft and light, almost … feathery…'

Mary could feel Percy's eyes blazing their disapproval at her clumsy wording, but Mary threw him a slight smile and he caught its meaning.

'No, you are wrong. She is petite, but she is strong. Her eyes are the colour of chestnuts, and her lips are full and wide. He is a washed-out cloud; she is the colour of the earth.'

Mary watched a dreamy expression float across Percy's face; he mouthed the words to himself before frantically scribbling them down.

'Here.' Madame Thibeaux relinquished her grip on the locket, pushing it quickly into Mary's hand with a speed that showed her reluctance to let it go. 'See for yourself.'

Mary looked at the image in the locket. She saw a well-defined face, inquisitive brown eyes framed by intelligent brows, full red lips, hair swept back in a respectable style; Madame Lamont was certainly a striking woman, and not one who could disappear easily.

'She is beautiful,' Mary said.

'She is.' Madame Thibeaux nodded.

Percy stepped over to Mary; she showed him the picture. 'She is possessed of fine features...' He cleared his throat and stepped back.

'You may keep that for your investigations, but I want it back when you find her.'

Madame Thibeaux sank further into her chair, exhaustion creasing her features. Mary needed to quicken her questions.

'Can you think of any reason she would want to disappear, or where she would go?'

'No. Claudine enjoys her life. I can see no reason why she would want to change it. Her husband can be a pig, it is true, but who can't? I bet even a handsome creature like you can have torrents of passion, *non*?'

Her gaze turned to Percy, challenging him with arched eyebrows and an expectant smile.

'Percy is a poet; he lives for torrents of passion!' Mary said with a laugh.

'Yes, I know.' She nodded; the parrot mimicked the action. 'I have read *Queen Mab*; it shows great promise, but there is work to be done.'

Mary watched for his reaction. Usually, Percy would flare up at the slightest hint of criticism and challenge the accuser to a battle of wits or weapons, but his only response was a light tapping of his foot upon the floor.

'Do not be angry that I have not praised every word. You are young, with a bright future ahead of you; perfection must be something constantly strived for and never attained. Take it from someone who has lived a long life.'

Percy's foot stopped tapping, and he smiled at Madame Thibeaux.

'So, you cannot think of any reason why Madame Lamont would voluntarily have left her home?' Mary pressed again.

'You should join our gendarmerie. You are like a terrier: once you get your teeth into something, you are impossible to shake off. You take after your mother.'

Mary's head snapped up. Madame Thibeaux's eyes glowed, and Mary saw a flash of familiar revolutionary zeal in them.

'You knew my mother?'

'I met her, only once, I'm afraid. She was quite a woman. I can see you have many of her characteristics.'

The mention of her mother brought tears to Mary's eyes. She felt her loss like a physical pain, a heavy grief that she would never trace their similarities for herself, nor see her own features in her mother's face. Mary put a hand to her chest.

'I am sorry, I did not mean to upset you, my dear. Here.' Madame Thibeaux passed Mary a handkerchief and she dabbed her eyes.

'*Allons, Allons!*' the parrot squawked sympathetically. Everyone laughed and the sadness evaporated like mist. Mary steered the conversation back to its former topic.

'Madame Thibeaux,' she whispered, 'what do you think has happened to Madame Lamont? If she was not in a mind to leave, is there a chance she was *made* to leave?'

'Made to leave? I could not say. There are plenty of foul places in Paris and foul people to occupy them. Claudine is a kind soul who feels things deeply. A foul deed against her … I cannot even think of the possibility. All I can hope is that she has taken herself off to the country for a couple of days.'

'I have heard that Parisians do that,' Percy contributed. 'Where would she go?'

'Most Parisians know where to go. As with anywhere, there are certain places to be seen and others to be hidden. If she wished to be seen then she would go to Giverny or Annecy, but if she did not wish to be seen, she would go to Troyes.'

CHAPTER TEN

Having collected Napoleon and Jane en route, Mary and Percy made their way back to Monsieur Lamont's offices; his room seemed all the dimmer after a morning spent in the bright sunshine. Lamont's complexion was greyer than the last time they had seen him and he had dark shadows under his eyes; his wife's disappearance was clearly taking its toll. He looked like he hadn't slept well in days.

Lamont ran a hand through his hair, which stuck up in spikes on the top of his head.

'We have been to Giverny and Annecy,' he said. 'Both have exceptional gardens, and Claudine is so fond of plants and trees. I have never heard of people going to Troyes. I cannot think why Madame Thibeaux suggested it. There is nothing there, no grand hotel. Nowhere comfortable.'

'You have been there?' Mary asked.

'Yes, I have stopped there for business, but it is not a place I visit often.' He paused and shook his head. 'I do not think it is a place Claudine has ever been.'

'That might make it the perfect place to try,' Percy ventured. Mary nodded.

'There are no coaches there. You must make your way on foot.'

'That is not a problem. We have our donkey now to carry our luggage or one of us if we are tired.'

'Perhaps you might need a second donkey?' Monsieur Lamont ventured.

Percy inhaled. Mary knew that money was a sensitive topic for him.

'Or a mule? Perhaps a mule to carry your luggage and the donkey for the journey?'

'Perhaps we shall, but we cannot afford to take rooms at Troyes. If you wish us to go there, you must secure the rooms for us.'

'I can do that. I shall contact the owner of the hotel and make bookings for — what — two rooms and a donkey?'

'That sounds agreeable,' Mary said. 'And the rooms will be paid for, to include meals and laundry?'

'Yes, I am sure we can come to some agreement about that.'

Mary nodded. She was growing accustomed to making big decisions.

'How is Napoleon doing?' Percy asked.

Mary had to run to catch up with him. He loved striding ahead into adventure, particularly when he did not know where he was going. She had tried to get him to plot out a route on the map as they had collected their things and prepared for the trip to Troyes, but he hadn't listened. According to her calculations, it should take approximately three days if they stuck to the main roads and took a direct route from Paris. She knew, however, that Percy's preference was for the scenic route, so although they had taken rooms at the imaginatively named Hotel de Troyes for a week from three days' time, she was glad she'd negotiated in an extra day in case of distractions or diversions. Monsieur Lamont assured her that Troyes was not the desirable tourist area they imagined and that they would probably find themselves to be the only people staying there.

'Napoleon is fine!' Jane shouted from behind them.

'You are sure we are going the right way?' Mary asked, trying her best to keep her tone even.

'We are going the only way, Mary!' Percy trilled, oblivious to any undercurrent of doubt she'd expressed.

She rubbed her lower back; all this walking made her back ache and the sickness that had plagued her at the start of their journey had made an unwelcome reappearance. With the relentless heat and scores of insects that seemed to make a sport of flying towards her face, she was soon feeling out of humour.

'Look over there!' he gasped, pointing to a forest that nudged away from the road. 'Do you think that will offer a more scenic route?'

Mary rolled her eyes inwardly; a scenic route meant a deviation from the main road and untold complications.

'Why don't you have a quick look at it while Jane, Napoleon and I rest here awhile and await your response?'

'A most capital idea!' he replied with a smile, bounding off enthusiastically.

Mary looked back towards Jane and Napoleon; their speed had slowed to a crawl. Jane wiped her forehead and looked thoroughly unhappy. Poor Napoleon was weighed down with their luggage.

'I do not know how he keeps his enthusiasm when it is so warm.' Jane fanned herself with her hands, turning to fan Napoleon too.

'I know. Ordinarily, it is an endearing trait of his, but in this circumstance, it is becoming a little tiresome.' Mary whispered the last word, not wanting Percy's enthusiasm to be dented by a lack of her own.

'Where has he gone?'

'Chasing perfection.' Mary sighed, then added quickly, 'He is looking for a more shaded route than this, I hope.'

'But the map showed this to be the more direct one.'

Mary pursed her lips. 'I know that, and you know that, but try telling that to Percy.'

'I am shrivelling up like a raisin in a desert.' Jane sighed heavily. 'Have we any water?'

Mary nodded, handing over the hipflask of water. Jane gulped loudly as she drank. Mary hoped she'd left some for everyone else.

'We should come to a farmhouse or two along the way; we can call in for shelter, milk and bread, but we will get little more than that until we reach Troyes.'

'I may be tempted to devour Napoleon's apples and carrots.'

Napoleon had sunk to the floor, the luggage spread out like a skirt around him. Mary couldn't imagine that he would move soon, and so they all sat down on the dusty pathway. Outside of the city, Paris was unassuming, and they had seen neither another person nor a house or farm in hours. They had left the hotel straight after an early breakfast while they still felt hardy, as Percy had said they would need to walk for most of the day in order to reach the first stop, but right now Mary could see nothing more than miles of endless, arid land taking them further away from civilisation, and bringing fire to their muscles and fatigue to their minds — hardly the optimum conditions for finding a missing person.

'I wonder if Percy is lost?' Mary said after an extended reverie. 'He has been gone for some time.'

'You see what is happening,' Jane replied. 'I will rest here with Napoleon.'

Typical, Mary thought. Usually Jane would leap at the chance for time alone with Percy, but now that Mary actually would prefer to sit quietly with the donkey and take a drink of water herself, that wasn't an option. She nodded, pulled up her skirts and walked off in the direction he'd taken earlier.

'Percy!' she yelled into the forest, shaking the birds from the trees. There was no response. 'Percy, come on, where are you? Now is not the time to be playing hide and seek.'

Mary circled around, looking up at the trees that dwarfed her and the patch of sky above, a milky blue against the lush vegetation which contrasted starkly with the dry paths they'd walked along.

'Percy!' she tried again, changing direction and moving towards a different space. She halted at a hidden furrow disguising a drop beneath it. 'Percy!' she cried, seeing his body sprawled out on the ground beneath. 'Oh no. Jane! Jane!' Within moments, Jane was at her side. 'Percy has fallen, look!'

Jane's hand rushed to her mouth, the colour vanishing from her face. 'Is he… Can we move him?'

A slight movement of Percy's arm brought indescribable relief to Mary, who burst into spontaneous tears.

'Oh, my love, Percy, are you all right? Are you hurt?'

Percy twisted on the ground, fragments of leaf and branches sticking to him as he rolled over.

'Yes, yes, I am… Ouch!' His face contorted with pain as he grabbed at his ankle.

'What is it? Is it broken?'

'I don't know,' he replied through gritted teeth. 'Help me up… Put me on that tree stump over there.'

His shaking finger pointed to a fallen tree trunk. Mary and Jane propped him up, an arm over each of their shoulders as he hopped over to the tree and sat down.

Mary rolled up his trouser leg and rolled down his stocking, then gently nudged his foot out of his shoe. The ankle was white and bulbous; it ballooned as soon as it hit the air. Mary knew there was no chance of getting the shoe back on.

'We must carry on.' Percy's pain punctuated each word. His face matched the phantom-white colour of his foot. 'I can walk it off.'

'You cannot walk off a broken ankle, Percy. What are we to do? Shall we turn back towards Paris? That would be easier than continuing on to Troyes,' Mary said.

'No.' Percy shook his head vehemently. 'We have promised Monsieur Lamont that we will continue our investigations in Troyes. Jane, bring Napoleon. I can hobble alongside him for now.'

Jane nodded and disappeared back to their previous spot. They heard her calling the donkey's name. It was no surprise when she reappeared alone.

'Napoleon has gone,' she said.

'Gone? What do you mean he's gone?' Mary asked.

'He's not where we left him.' Jane paced around. 'What are we to do?'

'He's a donkey — he won't have gone far. He hasn't come this way, so go and look up the road and see if you can find him.' Mary tried to remain calm; Percy and Jane's worried faces demanded it of her.

'What are we to do if she can't find him?' asked Percy once Jane had gone.

'We will have to head back to Paris.'

'And the missing wife?'

'Will have to stay missing. My immediate concern is for you, Percy, not her.' There was a sinking feeling in Mary's stomach that was telling her that this road led only back to London and her father's stern disapproval.

'I've found him!' Jane's relieved voice punctured the air. 'He had found a pool of water and was having a drink.'

Mary's mouth twitched at the remembrance of water, and she was overcome by a tremendous thirst.

'I wish I were a donkey,' Percy said, staring at an invisible sun. Delirium had quickly set in.

'Have a drink, Percy.' Mary passed him the hipflask and he drank until there was none left. Her own thirst would go unquenched then. 'Can you stand?'

He nodded and got unsteadily to his feet, and Mary shouldered his bodyweight as they made their way back to Jane and Napoleon.

'Right,' said Jane, 'how are we going to do this?'

'Percy is going on Napoleon with the lighter bags, and I'll carry the trunk.'

'You can't carry that alone, Mary; it is far too heavy for you,' Percy replied.

'It is fine. Jane, you can lead Napoleon, and I will drag this along. All will be well.' She tried to smile, but it was as weak and unconvincing as the sentiment behind it.

As Percy climbed onto Napoleon, Mary took a deep breath, picked up the handle of the trunk, and pulled it along. It was the last of her mother's things, her final material tie to her, and now it was being dragged along the dusty road like a corpse. They moved slowly, so slowly that even the delicate breeze outran them. Mercifully, the sun had faded, and the air was dry and hot but no longer humid — small mercies, Mary thought.

By dusk Mary was gripped by the delirium that had earlier gripped Percy and could hardly tell day from night. Sweat had dried on and re-soaked her garments so often that they were stiff and uncomfortable, and her back ached.

'There's a light over there, look,' Percy said. It was true. On a patch of land removed from the road was a single-storey building with a lamp in the window. Farmhouse or cowshed, that was where Mary was heading.

'Come on,' Mary urged, her enthusiasm temporarily restored by this potential reprieve from walking. They crossed over a field and then entered an area fenced off by a ramshackle wooden fence. The building was wooden, with a straw roof that whistled in the wind as they approached it. There did not seem to be any other buildings around, so Mary cautiously opened the door. Nothing but straw and hay, a bucket, and the overwhelming residual odour of animals.

'Hello?' she whispered into the gloom, half expecting a reply. Nothing.

A harsh wind ripped through the roof, which shook overhead.

'The wind is getting up. Let us stay here for the evening,' Percy said.

Mary and Jane nodded, helped Percy off Napoleon, and closed the door behind them. Mary lit the oil lamp. How long it would last was anyone's guess, and the thought of being in complete darkness — the sort of inky blackness Mary's monster could easily creep into — was unnerving.

'We may need to share Napoleon's nourishment this evening,' Percy continued, his words drowned out by a loud rumble from his stomach.

Jane handed each of them a carrot and an apple, which they ate greedily as if in a race. As they were out of water, they all took a sip from Percy's hipflask, the one with neat alcohol. Mary endured it, more for its numbing abilities than anything else.

'Let us try to make the best of it.' Mary pulled some straw from a bale and started assembling it on the floor like a bed. Jane did the same, making her own bed too close to theirs for

Mary's liking. A draught snuck in through a gap under the door, growling as it hit the airy room. Mary closed her eyes, unable to recall another night during which she had wished so fervently for the dawn.

'What are you doing in here?'

A voice accompanied by the clanging of a bucket woke them the next morning. A farmer stood in the doorway, the dirt on his face obscuring his expression. Percy, momentarily forgetting the pain in his ankle, hastened to sit up, slipping back down with a groan when he remembered. Mary, who had slept fitfully, was slower to respond, rubbing her eyes several times as if it would make the farmer disappear. Jane and Napoleon, side by side on the floor of the barn, continued to sleep.

'How did you get in?' the farmer asked.

'The … the door was open,' Mary stuttered.

The farmer's gaze turned towards her and softened. 'You must be hungry. Would you like something to eat?'

Mary and Percy exchanged a surprised glance. 'Yes, that would be most welcome. Thank you,' Percy said.

'Hurt yourself?' The farmer pointed at Percy's foot.

'Yes, I fell down and twisted my ankle.'

'I have a remedy for the pain. Perhaps you would like to wake your friends.' He nodded towards Jane and Napoleon.

Mary gently shook Jane awake. Jane still had hold of Napoleon's rein, clearly taking no chances after his recent escapades.

'Come on, Jane, we're going to have breakfast with… I'm sorry, what is your name?'

'Laurent — Laurent Osmond.'

'Good to meet you, Laurent. I'm Mary, this is Jane, and this is Percy.'

'The donkey? The donkey is Percy?' Laurent frowned.

'No, the man is Percy. The donkey is…' She hesitated; how would Napoleon Bonaparte's defeat be received in rural Paris? Mary thought it best not to mention it. 'The donkey is … Donkey.' She nodded to Jane and Percy to stay tight-lipped.

'Well, you are all welcome in the farmhouse. It is not much, but it is warm and dry.'

They thanked him and followed him up to the farmhouse, Napoleon braying at the birds, who sang a sweet dawn chorus in response.

Several hours later, fortified by a hearty breakfast and with replenished water bottles and a natural arnica treatment for Percy's ankle, they walked in the direction Laurent had suggested as a more pleasant, easier route to Troyes. The swelling in Percy's ankle had reduced, and he could now put his foot into his shoe. Laurent told them of a stream two fields hence, which was next to another stable where they could rest. Since the Sixth coalition's troops of Austrian, Prussian and Russian forces had invaded the countryside on their march through to Troyes, slaughtering the animals they had no use for and taking those they did, there was not much call for the stables at present. On leaving, Percy had surreptitiously placed some gold Napoleon coins on the table, sensing that the farmer would be much too proud to accept them in exchange for his kindness.

By the following day, they were almost back on schedule. Troyes, a hotel and a bed with a mattress seemed tantalisingly close.

'Mary,' Percy called from atop Napoleon, most of his previous zest restored, 'let us consider everything we know about Madame Lamont.'

'The general impression we have gleaned so far is that she is kind and shy, prefers nature to people, is careful with her friends and happy with her life,' Mary replied.

'Did you get the impression that Madame Thibeaux was trying to hide something?' Percy asked. Mary, who was leading the donkey while Jane took a turn pulling the trunk, stopped.

'No.' She shook her head. 'But I'm sensing that you did.'

'She was quick to talk about trapped birds and gilded cages, but I got the impression she was talking more of her own experience than Madame Lamont's.'

'That's as may be, but we cannot take that as proof that she is hiding something.'

'Perhaps you are right; perhaps I am just being cynical.' Percy sighed. Mary clicked the rein and Napoleon started walking again.

'What reason would Madame Thibeaux have to lie about anything?' Mary asked after a moment.

'She might have helped Madame Lamont to make her escape.'

CHAPTER ELEVEN

A row of peasant farmers lined the streets of Troyes, watching them.

Mary scarcely registered their arrival. The journey had been disappointing. Farmer Osmond's attempt to secure them a more scenic route showed that his idea of a scenic route was wildly different to hers. A succession of dusty landscapes stripped of all greenery welcomed them; what trees there were had scarred trunks and branches and shook angry fists of dried leaves as they passed by. The land wore the same battle scars that had adorned the countryside on their way into Paris, and was populated by the same suspicious-looking farmers who now viewed Percy's arrival on a donkey with amusement, hiding their mirth behind their hands and talking in a dialect Mary couldn't quite place and at a speed she could not keep up with.

The hotel itself was hardly more impressive than the farmer's stable, though at least Mary and Percy would have their own room, away from Jane and Napoleon. This was a great mercy, as Jane had not carried the trunk with the same magnanimity as Mary, huffing and puffing with each step, and narrating her feelings as if she were on stage performing a soliloquy. Once they had eaten a frugal meal, they were all glad to go their separate ways and enjoy a night hopefully more restful than its predecessors.

'What a time we are having, Mary.' Percy collapsed onto the bed, exhaustion etched on his features. In the dim light, he looked older than his twenty-two years. 'Did you ever think when you agreed to come away with me that you would sleep in a barn, carry trunks across hillocks and make friends with a donkey?'

'When you put our achievements in a roll call like that, it sounds unimaginable!'

'I feel like I made promises to you that I have not fulfilled. By accelerating our relationship, I have derailed it…'

Percy cast a mournful glance at the ground. Mary smiled. She was entirely wise to this trick of his, the forlorn lover fishing for reassurance that could only be granted in the sweetness of kisses and declarations of love. His emotions were only superficial; Mary knew that her own ran much deeper. The practical decisions she had undertaken so far on their journey had stamped out much of her youthful optimism, making her feel dull and plain and practically middle-aged. Sweeping her own feelings to one side, she attended to his.

'Now, Percy, why should you feel that way? A relationship is strengthened by adversity. If it crumbles under its weight, then it is too weak to last. Our adversities have hardened my resolve and deepened my affections, not diminished them.'

Percy brightened and motioned for Mary to join him on the bed. He cupped her face in his hands. 'My own precious lily, my nymph…'

He kissed her neck. Desire stirred inside her, hummed through her body like a familiar song. She closed her eyes, lack of sleep sending her into a delicious daze which dulled her senses and made her soar out of her body, watching the scene from above, taking it all in — there but not there. Percy unbuttoned his nightgown, exposing his taut, youthful flesh, which showed no signs of his internal conflict. He unbuttoned hers and their moon-milk whiteness glowed in the half-light as their bodies entwined wordlessly, with natural symmetry. As he pressed himself within her, a wave of desire engulfed her, drowning her in passion until all she could hear was her heart pounding loudly — it seemed to call her name, quietly at first and then more determinedly. But now it wasn't just calling her name, it was shaking the door.

The door swung open to reveal Jane standing in the doorway with a candle in her hand.

'Oh my... Jane!' Mary pushed Percy away, gathering the sheets up to her chin. 'Jane, what are you doing? Go back to bed!' Mary's eyes bulged.

'I am not setting foot in that room. A cockroach just ran across my face.'

'A cockroach? I am sure it was not a cockroach.'

Percy jumped out of bed, his naked body a white stripe in the gloom. Jane stared at him for a beat too long before turning her gaze away.

'Jane, I am sure it was nothing more than a woodlouse, or perhaps a beetle.' Percy put an arm around her, ushering her into the bedroom. Mary pulled the sheet higher as Percy and Jane sat down on the end of the bed.

'Look, one is on the sole of my shoe! I am sure there are many others.'

Jane took her shoe off and Percy examined it. Mary huffed. She was clearly the only one to value privacy and discretion. Percy and Jane analysed the dead insect as if it were a fascinating new discovery by Pierre André Latreille.

'Would you feel better if I checked the room before you return to sleep in it?'

'I tell you now that I shall get no sleep in that room. All I will hear is that incessant scuttling — it makes me shudder to think of it.' Jane shivered.

'Well, you cannot stay here. Let us see if we can get you another room. One with no additional occupants?' Mary pulled her arm into her nightdress.

'I have already tried that.' Jane sighed. 'There is nowhere, nothing to be had.'

'If Percy goes to check, will you stay there, then?' Mary asked.

'Yes. I will accompany him and show him where it was,' Jane replied. 'There may be more.'

Mary watched her stepsister ogling Percy as he dressed. He himself seemed blissfully unaware of the emotions he was stirring. Mary sighed. She would have to contain this jealousy if she were truly to take part in Percy's utopian ideal. It didn't do to show any signs of resentment or ownership. They must be squashed, like the cockroach.

'Do not keep him too long. I am keen to resume our previous … discussion.' Mary winked at Percy, who raised an eyebrow in response. Good to remind Jane who was in his bed and in his heart. Percy and Jane left the room, closing the door loudly behind them, the thud quickly replaced by the sound of their laughter echoing down the corridor.

The room felt cold and empty without him, as if a great fire had gone out. Was that how it felt to be out of Percy's favour? If so, it wasn't a feeling she liked. Distractedly, she picked up her mother's book, *Letters Written in Sweden, Norway and Denmark*, flicking through the pages in the half-light, trying to concentrate on her mother's words as if they were a balm to her soul. It was no use. Jealousy consumed her mind and no matter how hard she tried, she could not rest. Mary threw the book down on the bed and breathed deeply.

After lying in the darkness for what seemed like an eternity, the chirping birds alerted her to the dawn. Opening her eyes, she realised that sleep had begrudgingly swept in when least expected. Her hand lay on the book's cover, but the other side of the bed was cold and empty.

Jane was particularly smug and superior at breakfast, but Percy's demeanour was unchanged. Though Mary's brain raced with the urge to ask what had prevented his return to their room, she knew that would bring nothing but reprisals from Jane and throw Percy into a sulk. It didn't do to harbour jealousies. Percy wouldn't like it. Jane was here — that was a fact she could do little about — but the adventure was chiefly theirs. Mary and Percy were the team, Jane little more than a sidekick. As long as the dynamic stayed that way, there was nothing to concern herself with.

Breakfast completed, they asked the hotel proprietor if there were any more hotels in the area and were astounded to learn that there were. Ones that he conceded were more suited to rich patrons, even going so far as to express surprise that people of their social standing should honour his establishment with their presence. Mary felt stung that Monsieur Lamont had forced them to endure this one; it was a double blow to discover that there was now more work to be done in trying to locate Madame Lamont in Troyes.

'We will need to locate all the hotels. Then, we must put together a list and talk to the proprietors to see if anyone matching Madame Lamont's name or description has checked in. Do you still have her likeness?' Percy nodded. 'Jane can rest at the hotel with Napoleon. If she is bored, she may take him for a walk. She must be exhausted after the cockroach commotion last night.'

There was not a flicker on Percy's face, but then, there wouldn't be. Mary wanted nothing more than to ask him directly if he had been intimate with Jane, but the words would not leave her lips. His having told her he had divested the room of insects was as close as she would get to a satisfactory response, and she would just have to learn to live with that. If she couldn't, then surely she could not stay in a relationship which required her to become such a hypocrite. The thought of losing him entirely was like being suddenly plunged into a freezing river and left to drown. Her entire body felt immobile, unresponsive. She *could* learn to live with it; she *would* learn to live with it. Percy was talking, oblivious to Mary's distraction.

'I spoke to the proprietor about Jane's room this morning. She is to be moved onto a different floor.'

'That is good news,' Mary said with a smile.

'So, you and I shall visit the hotels and then this afternoon perhaps we can resume our *discussion* in our room?'

Mary softened. 'Let us endeavour to get our answers quickly!'

The town centre of Troyes was nothing like the route they had taken to the hotel. The cobbled streets held a rustic, ramshackle charm that was probably easily missed by tourists seeking grandiosity and wealth but spun a gentle, magical spell on Mary, whose mind weaved stories into each dusty passageway, each narrow street. Having come from London, with all its vastness, small towns held great appeal for her, and this town was proud of all the different aspects of its identity. Pockets of the town wore its patriotism in buildings draped with coats of arms and finery, and colourful, half-timbered houses were clustered in petite rows. It was easy to see why it attracted the people who wanted to conceal themselves; there were plenty of hiding places.

'There is a hotel.' Percy pointed to the end of the cobbled street. 'And there is another over there. I will enquire at the first, while you go to the other. We will meet under the clock tower.'

Mary nodded. 'That sounds agreeable. Good luck!'

Half an hour later, she was waiting for Percy to come back from his investigations. When he did, his cheeks were ruddy, and he walked with a slight swagger caused by his injured ankle.

'Anything?'

'No.' He hiccupped. 'But the owner insisted on giving me a small glass of claret as a welcome. Did you get anything?'

'Sadly, no, not even an offer of claret.' Mary shook her head. 'A couple of names of the best places to be seen, but nothing of the places one might go to disappear. Perhaps we will do better if we investigate together?'

Percy smiled as Mary took his arm and they walked across the cobbled streets.

'I have always been a fan of Gothic churches.' Mary stared up at the spire of a church in the distance, its roof bowed into a curve that reminded her of a priest's hood. 'Let us look at the churches and the hotels. We know nothing of Madame Lamont's religion — she may be devout for all we know.'

'Perhaps she has found God and has run away to join a nunnery. Or she is hiding in a hotel, undertaking a deliciously salacious affair,' Percy said with a smirk. Anything involving passion was always his preference.

'Perhaps both, simultaneously,' Mary said evenly. Percy's face betrayed the fact that he hadn't understood her joke. 'Oh, Percy, I am not being serious!'

'Oh.' His face fell.

'Percy, look!' Mary suddenly elbowed him in the ribs. 'Does that woman over there not match Claudine Lamont's description?'

Percy squinted at the retreating figure. 'I don't know. It is hard to see from here.'

'Then let us speed up after her.'

Mary quickened her pace, racing along the cobbles, Percy struggling to keep up with her. The woman was dressed in a plain dress, her dark hair tied up in an efficient, nondescript style designed to blend in rather than garner attention. Atop it was an unfashionable hat chosen for practical rather than aesthetic reasons. *A very sensible-looking woman*, Mary thought. It had to be her. She walked with a buoyant step — the step of someone unconcerned with onlookers, or someone in a hurry. As she crossed the street, Mary stayed a couple of steps behind, watching as the woman approached a café. Percy hobbled towards Mary.

'Mary.' He struggled to catch his breath. 'Please stop running off like that. I cannot keep up and I am not about to try. If you wish me to run at such speeds, then we must bring Napoleon for me to ride on.'

'Sorry, sorry.' Mary hushed him, then inclined her head towards the café and the table at the front, where the woman was now seated.

'There she is,' she said. 'What should we do now?'

CHAPTER TWELVE

'How about going up to her and asking her if she is Madame Lamont?' suggested Percy.

'Just like that?'

Percy nodded. 'Yes, just like that.'

'Perhaps she does not want to be found?'

'Perhaps she is having a delightful holiday and just forgot to tell her husband about it?' Percy shrugged. 'It is possible. I have frequently got carried along with some adventure and forgotten to tell … people … where I was.'

He means his wife, Harriet, Mary thought. The unspoken smudge on their perfect union.

'I would not dream of leaving without at least a note.' She felt a pang at the memory of the note she had left for her father and how little it had done to repair the rift between them. 'Any respectable woman would do the same.' A generalisation. She was angry that she knew so much about society, or that she knew enough to show that she was concerned by it. When had she become so … conventional? Her judgements were stacking up like pebbles.

'I will talk to her. Wait here.'

Mary stayed back as Percy made his way across to the café. She saw the woman frown and then smile as Percy spoke to her, the shake of her head when he asked a question, and the way she watched him as he walked back. A flicker of jealousy ignited inside her. Would it always be like this? Would there be danger in every glance, every woman a potential threat to the delicate balance of their harmony? Could his head be as easily swayed by another as it had been by her? Mary sighed. She hoped not.

'Well?' asked Mary.

'She says that she is not Madame Lamont, but that I was the second person to ask such. She will talk to us if you want to ask her more questions.'

'Really? I wonder who the other person was?' Mary turned her gaze back to the café. The table where the woman had sat was empty. 'Oh.'

Mary's spirits sank. For a moment she had felt as though they were getting somewhere, but now they were back to square one. If the woman wasn't Madame Lamont, then why had she left the café so abruptly?

'Did she tell you her name?' Mary prayed Percy had at least uncovered some further detail about her.

'I'm afraid not.' Percy shook his head. 'I feel stupid for not asking, but once she said she was willing to talk to us, I thought I would fetch you directly.'

'Yes, I understand that.' Mary sighed. 'Never mind. Let us try some more hotels to see if they have seen either Madame Lamont or her lookalike; at least now I feel able to give a more accurate description of her.' There would be no going back to the hotel before suppertime. 'Come along, Percy.'

The search for the two Madame Lamonts was fruitless and by the end of their search, Mary and Percy had begun to believe that the woman they had seen outside the café was nothing but a figment of their imagination. They approached the last hotel on their list with a mixture of trepidation and fatigue, seating themselves at a table in front of the establishment, which overlooked the cobbled courtyard and the elevated church. Unwelcome afternoon heat stifled the air, the glare of the sun bouncing off the cobbles. Percy used the map to fan himself while Mary kept a watchful eye on the street, keen to pounce on the woman from the café should she walk past again.

'I don't know if I could do this full-time,' Percy stated, the map wilting as he wafted it. 'Chasing around after people is exhausting.'

'So is poverty, my dear,' Mary countered, accepting the sole glass of water that had made up their order.

All around them, locals continued with café life, untouched by the recent battles — huddled together in conversations, laughing conspiratorially over croissants and coffee. This was a place with none of the defeated bashfulness of the countryside, nor the hard, worn faces of the farmers whose land and livelihood had been ripped up and destroyed. Here, skin and eyes shone healthily as if the previous worries had floated on past this town like tumbleweed, but the clothes were out of fashion and the coffee cups chipped. This was not a place for people to preen and parade themselves.

Mary looked around; they seemed out of place, but not uncomfortably so. People were neither falling over themselves to serve them nor hostile to their presence; they were served with a laconic, universal politeness but nothing more. Yes, it would be easy to hide yourself away here. They sat and watched as the sun streaked through the stained-glass window in the church steeple, splashing the pebbles with puddles of colour. A man at the next table dropped a copy of the *Gazette de France* as he left. Mary picked it up.

'I suppose I should ask the proprietor if he knows of a Madame Lamont, or if anyone has recently asked after her,' said Percy.

'Capital,' Mary replied. 'And I shall scour the *Gazette* for any news from Paris.'

Percy soon returned to the table, brandishing a telegram. 'This was left for me at reception: it is a message from Madame Thibeaux, but why would she be sending a message to us at this hotel? We are not staying here.'

CHAPTER THIRTEEN

'Why would Madame Thibeaux send it here? Perhaps she knows that we will check all the hotels; perhaps we would find the same message at every one.' Mary tapped her fingers on the table. 'What does it say?'

'It says: *Return to Paris immediately. I have news.*'

Mary sat back in her chair. 'I wonder what the news could be?'

'Perhaps she has heard from Madame Lamont?' Percy offered.

'No.' Mary shook her head. 'If there was any news from Paris, surely we would have heard it from Monsieur Lamont.'

'It is possible that Madame Thibeaux got in touch with him following our conversation with her. Perhaps between them they have re-doubled their efforts and solved their own mystery, leaving us redundant and penniless.' Percy huffed and ran his hand through his hair. 'I have nothing else to sell except Napoleon, and without him we have no means of transportation at all.'

'There are bankers here, are there not? Is it not worth trying to see if the name Percy Shelley carries any sway here?'

'If it cannot secure finance in Paris, it is unlikely to secure funds here.'

'It is worth a try, though, and we need to make plans if we are to return to Paris.'

'Why don't you and Jane return to Paris while Napoleon and I stay here and try our luck with the bankers?'

Mary folded her arms but said nothing. The thought of long days making idle conversation with Jane made her spirits sink.

But at least it took Jane out of Percy's immediate attentions, and as his ankle was not wholly restored, it made sense for him to keep the donkey with him. It would also give her the opportunity to interrogate Jane regarding what really happened the other night.

'All right, we shall gather supplies today and set off first thing tomorrow morning.' Mary's voice was firm; she was glad to have some sort of plan.

'Let us walk around Troyes and sketch out potential recipients for my begging bowl,' Percy suggested with a smile.

Back at the hotel, they immediately sought Napoleon, finding him well and enjoying a shaded area in the hotel's field. They went to check on Jane. She had spent the afternoon reading and was in a state of repose, transported into a dreamy haze by the romantic words of Byron.

'Do you think you shall ever meet him, Percy?' she asked. Mary detected more than a hint of optimism behind her eyes. 'I would so like to meet the author of *Childe Harold's Pilgrimage.*'

'He is a great poet and a very famous one.' Percy sighed. 'I am not in Byron's league; I doubt our poetic paths shall ever cross.'

'You are a great poet, Percy, and you will be a famous one. You just need to give it time,' Mary replied soothingly.

'Thank you, Mary, but I feel that perhaps your love for me clouds your artistic judgement. I need a sober, more impartial critic — Napoleon, perhaps.'

'If ever a donkey deserved a sonnet, it is he,' said Mary, agreeing. 'But pleasant though this talk of poetry is, Jane, we come to entreat you to join us in a plan.'

Jane's face lit up. 'I love a plan,' she said, rubbing her hands together so vigorously that Mary feared she would catch fire. 'Tell me all.'

The rudiments of the plan established, Jane nodded as she processed all that Mary had said. 'And we are to walk there and back, without taking the coach?'

'Yes.'

Jane groaned. Percy looked at Mary, who shrugged.

'However,' said Percy, waving a finger in the air, 'if I can successfully conclude my business here within a couple of days, myself and Napoleon will return to Marais and meet you back at the hotel. We can use the last of our money to secure rooms and implore Monsieur Lamont to provide more funds when we report back to him. Hopefully, I will have secured an advance from a banker here.'

'We are setting great store by hopes.' Jane folded her arms. 'It feels as though we are stepping from one disaster into another.'

Percy's face crumpled. Mary put a sympathetic arm out to him, cursing Jane inwardly. There was so much pressure and expectation on him and so little that she or Jane could do — that society would allow them to do. He had shouldered so much already in his young life — marriage, parenthood, another child on the way with a woman he did not love. That knot was back, twisting at her stomach again, dampening the situation with heavy doses of reality.

Jane looked remorseful. 'Sorry, Percy, I did not mean that. When I am tired, I speak without thinking. Forgive me.'

'Sometimes I think we should just sail back to England and cut our losses. We are only prolonging our misery by stretching it out over continents,' Percy said with a sigh.

A faraway look clouded his eyes, as if the weight of the world had suddenly pressed itself on him. Mary much preferred the sunny expression that accompanied a poem or an act of love. Mary worried about him in these moments, how closed-off he became, isolating himself from everyone around him. It was impossible to reach him at such times. She feared that one day he would drift so far off course that it would be impossible to bring him back. For now, he snapped back out of it with just a peck on the cheek and a ruffle of his curls.

'There can be no misery with you, my love,' Mary soothed. 'Only adventure.'

Mary and Jane said goodbye to Percy and Napoleon and made their way back into the dusty countryside, where the sun was ripening the ground. Each carried supplies enough for the three-day walk back to Paris and Mary, trusting no one's sense of direction except her own, carried the map.

She sped ahead, keen to keep a good pace and arrive in Paris before they were expected. Jane followed quietly behind, saying nothing, which was preferable to the complaints with which she'd peppered the previous leg of their journey. Without the luggage, donkey and an injured Percy, it was peaceful, and Mary didn't mind the uneven pathways. She needed to keep a clear head and a safe footing — everything else was secondary.

They finally stopped to rest when Mary's calves burned with reluctance to go any further. Troyes was a distant blur behind them and their view now was almost entirely yellow — they were back in the sand-strewn rural area, where everything felt broken and torn. Peasant farmers in dusty caps stared at them with gummy grins, laughing at the spectacle of two Englishwomen dressed in black stomping like a pair of overgrown magpies across the countryside. One shouted to them that they needed a man and a mule, and Mary resisted the temptation to provide an acerbic retort. They stopped at a small stream in a clearing.

'Mary, look at that! That is exactly what I need. It's as if the gods have put it there for our use!' Jane stripped down to her undergarments and was preparing to shed those when Mary shouted to her.

'Please remain clothed! I am about to eat and the sight of your flesh will put me off my bread and ham.'

Jane splashed water in Mary's direction; it landed on the bank in front of her. 'Very well,' she sighed. 'I shall only go in up to my knees and keep modest attire at all times.'

Mary straightened her back, unwrapped her food and averted her eyes from Jane, focusing instead on the birds practising their formations in the sky above. A flock of starlings circled in perfect synchronicity — except for one bird who deviated away from the rest, whose movements did not match the perfect beats of the others. Mary's heart flew up to the bird and she willed it to carry on, to have faith that everything would happen in its own time. She looked back at Jane — which of them was the lone bird in their situation? Mary, for trying to start a life with Percy when she hadn't truly formed a life of her own? Or Jane, who didn't even have the security of romance to help her navigate the tempestuous waters in which she swam?

'You should come in, Mary. The water is lovely.' Jane's smile was wide and open, all her usual affectations discarded along with her clothes. Perhaps if she could be more uninhibited like Jane, Mary thought, they could be friends and there would be no disharmony between them.

'I will come and refresh my face, but nothing more,' Mary replied, putting her food down and meandering over to the water's edge. As she got there, she heard heavy wings flapping down and saw a raven — a swift ink smudge against the grassy bank — pick up her bread and take it up into the sky.

'You can share mine,' Jane said with a laugh. This time, when she flicked the water towards Mary, it landed on the skirt of her gown.

Mary laughed. 'This makes me think of childhood summers,' she sighed, taking off her shoes and tights and dipping her toes into the water. 'When summers seemed to stretch for a year and the world seemed endlessly emerald.'

'Endlessly emerald.' Jane nodded. 'I like that. Do not write that in your journal, otherwise Percy will steal it for a poem.'

'We share our ideas as much as everything else,' Mary replied. She had not meant to ensnare Jane into a conversation about Percy, but now the words had passed her lips, there was no retracting them.

'Well, it is good to share, is it not? We can never truly own or be owned. Percy told me that. It is not in keeping with his philosophy.'

Mary nodded, trying to swallow down the lump in her throat. The question hovered on the tip of her tongue like a blade.

'You asked me to tell you how it felt to make love to him. I ask you now, and answer me truthfully, have you now had the same experience?'

Jane hesitated. 'You are talking about the night of the cockroaches, I presume?'

Mary's thoughts swam around her head. Now she had given her jealousy the rein, it galloped through her and would not be stopped. All she could do was nod.

'I know you do not believe us when we say that nothing happened, but nothing did.'

'And would you tell me, truthfully, if it did?'

'I would tell you, yes. Would I share every detail with you? Truthfully, no.' Jane stepped out of the water. 'There seems to be a sudden chill in the air, don't you think? Perhaps we should keep moving.'

Mary watched her as she stepped back into her clothes. Jane was so comfortable with her own body that Mary couldn't help but feel reserved and old-fashioned in contrast. Perhaps of their natures, Jane's was the most closely aligned with Percy's. Mary tried to be liberal and to pay no heed to convention or society's rules, but just like clothes, social conventions were difficult to discard. If he had not noticed it already, how long would it be before Percy saw Jane as a better match?

'I will say one thing.' Jane stopped buttoning up her dress. 'If anything will dampen his feelings, it is jealousy and possessiveness. I would be wary of exhibiting those traits.'

Despite the chill, Mary felt a surge of heat rush through her. There was no way she was taking relationship advice from Jane.

'When you have a relationship of your own and are no longer invading mine, I shall take advice from you; until then, accept your place. You invited yourself on this trip; your company was not sought by me or Percy, and you will do well to remember that.'

Mary picked up their belongings and walked ahead, her eyes fixed on the horizon, not trusting herself to even look at Jane. When she thought of all they had given her, a life so much better than the one she would have had in London, she felt as dark and thunderous as the clouds that had slowly rolled into the sky, obscuring the sunshine with a grey, sinister air, as if concealing something. She had the same feeling about Jane, as if one day the mask of amity would slip and something would happen that would sever their relationship entirely. Judging by Jane's keenness to put distance between them, she felt sure the mistrust flowed in both directions.

They walked on for miles, the silence punctuated by the occasional buzzing insect or the snapping of twigs as they moved through the forests. The land alternated between arid, open terrain and the hidden enclaves of trees, but common to both were a lack of people or houses. By the time night fell, they were back at Farmer Osmond's barn and took their place once again amongst the straw. Mary took a space as far away from Jane as she could manage, and after a small meal of bread and cheese, she settled down to sleep.

Percy had taken Napoleon with him for the tour of the Troyes bankers. At first, he had thought it a good way to exercise the donkey but then, noting that the rejections were kinder with a donkey in tow, he decided that Napoleon's big teeth and doleful eyes might induce more favourable responses and possibly financial advancements. Napoleon was a good sidekick, braying enthusiastically, allowing himself to be stroked, and gently nuzzling at hands that offered carrots or hay. By the time they reached the third bank, Percy had almost forgotten his chief aim was to obtain money, so pleasant was it to be making conversation unrelated to Madame Lamont. He was enjoying the gentle time spent walking with a donkey in the sunshine, and words danced through his mind like woodland nymphs. It was the first time he'd felt remotely inspired since they'd arrived in Troyes.

He was regretting his spontaneity. He wasn't regretting the elopement, not a bit, but he had conceded that perhaps better financial planning and insight might have saved them from this sorry situation. Paris had not lived up to his expectations either. He'd been expecting a city full of revolutionary zeal, all colour and noise and people who shared his philosophy — not a city on its knees. It was hard to believe that so much had changed since Mary Wollstonecraft's visit. But it wasn't all bad. He and Mary had finally lived as man and wife, and that alone was worth all the stresses and strains.

They made their way to a café in the centre, Napoleon treading delicately on the cobbles, his hooves upright like a ballerina *en pointe*. Everywhere he went, solemn faces broke into smiles at the sight of him; Percy could only wish to garner so much attention. The final round of bankers was in sight, but only after they'd stopped for a drink.

'A coffee for me and a water and a carrot for my donkey, please,' Percy said.

The waiter smiled, bowed his head and scurried away, returning with a bucket of water from which Napoleon gratefully drank. Percy's coffee followed minutes later, and he stretched back in his chair, watching as the town of Troyes played out its daily rhythms around him. A farmer walked past, dragging an unwilling cow to market. For some reason, his thoughts turned to Mary and Jane. He wondered how they were getting on with their walk back to Paris. In another day, they would be back there and finding out what was behind Madame Thibeaux's urgent message, and perhaps he would have secured the money that would enable them to put this situation behind them and get back to the business of travelling in style and comfort.

Percy turned back to the table. He paused. The water bucket was upturned, and Napoleon had gone. Had he been so preoccupied with his own thoughts that he hadn't heard Napoleon untie himself? A cold thought flashed through his mind. Perhaps Napoleon hadn't untied himself, but had been untied. He had been stolen. Percy jumped up, knocking his chair over. He rushed to return it to its previous position just as the café owner came out with upturned hands and a scowl on his face, uttering words that Percy didn't quite understand and definitely didn't want to.

'My donkey, it has gone,' Percy stuttered in broken French.

The café owner looked at him quizzically. Percy gestured frantically towards the space Napoleon had vacated — surely the bucket would give it away? The man's eyes narrowed; he clearly thought this was little more than a ruse to get out of paying the bill. Percy sighed, flicked the coins onto the table and walked away. He stopped a little further down the road beside the clock tower and looked this way and that, hoping for some sign of Napoleon, but the streets were empty. He scratched his head. If Napoleon had gone voluntarily, where would he go? Somewhere he could get food. The market.

Percy hobbled down the road to the market and sure enough, there was Napoleon, his rein in the hand of a ruddy-faced farmer wearing a straw hat that looked like a sunshade. Napoleon was nudging and pulling at the rein. Percy went over to them. When the donkey saw Percy, he stopped pulling. Percy stroked the donkey's back.

'Thank goodness for that. I was beginning to think I had lost you.'

'Is this your donkey?' the farmer asked, his knuckles tightening on the rein.

'Yes, it is.'

'And how do I know that?' The man looked at Percy and then Napoleon with narrowed eyes.

'You don't, but it is of no concern to you at all. This is my donkey, and that is all there is to it. Kindly give me the rein.' Percy held out his hand.

The farmer hesitated, then shook his head. 'No,' he said, flatly. 'I don't think I will do that. This is my donkey.'

'This is not your donkey. This is my donkey; he's just escaped from the café up the road.'

'The café up the road? What was he doing there, reciting poetry?' the farmer said loudly, looking round at the other farmers who had gathered around them, closing in on Percy. They all laughed. Percy and Napoleon were outnumbered.

'Look, I don't want to get into a fight, but this is my donkey, and I am taking him back with me now.' Percy's voice shook as he spoke. He despised bullies and crowds, and this was the very worst of each of those.

'Excuse me,' said a woman's voice, breaking through the crowd, 'are those your cows in that pen at the back? The pen is wide open.'

The farmer who was holding Napoleon's rein let it go and gestured to his friends. They made for the back of the market, all thoughts of Napoleon forgotten. As the crowd dispersed, Percy saw the woman more clearly. It was the same woman from the café, the woman who looked like Madame Lamont.

'I think they will forget about your donkey now,' she said with a laugh.

Percy gripped Napoleon's rein. 'Thank you for that. I wasn't sure how I was going to get out of it.'

'No problem.' She smiled. She was dressed differently today; her clothes were older and worn, work clothes. 'I am sorry I disappeared the other day. I had to go to work.' She smoothed down her skirt with her hands.

'I was worried that I'd somehow scared you off.'

'No.' She shook her head. 'I was just late, that is all. My name is Pascale.'

'Percy. Percy Shelley.'

'Well, Percy, it was nice to see you again. Now, I really must go, otherwise I will be late again.'

'Where do you work?' Percy asked.

Pascale stepped back, her brow furrowed.

'I apologise. It is none of my business. It is just that myself and my … friends … are investigating the disappearance of a woman named Madame Lamont, and you said that someone had made the same mistake as I, stopping you because you look like her?'

'That is right, they did. A woman.'

'A woman?' Percy's mind raced through the possibilities. 'I don't suppose she told you her name or her connection to Madame Lamont?'

'It was at the market.' Pascale tapped her lips with her fingers. 'I think she said she was Madame Lamont's cook. She looked very surprised to see me. That's all I can tell you.' She turned away. 'I'm sorry, but I really must go now.'

A loud commotion at the back of the market showed that the farmer had got the cows back. They mooed loudly, shuffling despondently back into the pen. The farmer shot a glance in Percy's direction.

'I must go too, before they come back for Napoleon. I'll walk with you.'

Mary and Jane finally arrived back in Paris just as dawn was breaking over the banks of the Seine. Though their legs ached, and their spirits dragged, neither had shared their thoughts with the other, preferring to keep up the silent hostility, even if they could no longer remember its cause.

Unable to afford the rooms in their previous hotel, they settled for a cheaper hotel in the Latin Quarter near to the tavern in which Mary and Percy had learnt of Monsieur Lamont's secret task. It was no better in daylight, the buildings casting shadows on street corners where only intermittent whistles warned them of strangers ahead. Mary pulled her luggage close; she couldn't afford to lose that. She was regretting the loss of Napoleon; her shoulders were heavy, and she wanted to close her eyes and sleep for weeks. But that wasn't why they were here. There was work to be done.

For economy's sake, and for no other reason, Mary and Jane were sharing a room. The hotel owner insisted on showing them up himself, taking great pains to point out all the architectural features they passed. Mary's eye was drawn more to the patches of damp on the ceiling, the peeling wallpaper and the half-broken sconces that lined the wall and warned them that they couldn't rely on these lamps to light their way. Once night fell, they needed to be in their room and not leave it for any reason.

'And here is the room,' said the hotelier with a dramatic flourish it really didn't merit.

Mary glanced at Jane. Fear momentarily united them.

'You will provide candles or lanterns?' Jane asked, coughing to keep her voice even. Mary could sense the tremor beneath it.

'We can,' said the hotelier. 'But they will cost extra. You can use your own if you have them.'

'Is there an establishment nearby where we can purchase them?'

The man shook his head. 'No, but I can rent you some.'

'If you can rent them, then you can provide them gratis,' Mary said firmly.

Something in her expression must have startled him, for he stepped back, almost colliding with the bed.

He nodded. 'I am sure we can arrange something. Now, I must leave you while I check on the other rooms.'

He closed the door behind him, a faint twitch pulsing through his hand.

'That was strange,' Jane said. 'I don't know why he was so terrified of you.'

'Perhaps I reminded him of his wife.' Mary shrugged. 'I don't know about you, but I'm not leaving anything of value here.' Not that their luggage was stuffed full of jewels or money. The only things she would not leave behind were the journals she and Percy had been writing, and those of her mother. 'Let us refresh ourselves and go to Madame Thibeaux's.'

Clothes changed and faces washed, Mary was relieved to be free of the sticky sweat that had accompanied her on the journey, even if the stifling heat of Paris had brought back her sickness. They wove themselves through streets Mary had seen before, but they were new to Jane, and she kept stopping to marvel at the sights. Not for the first time, Mary wished she'd brought the donkey instead.

They arrived at Madame Thibeaux's in the middle of the morning. Mary hoped the elderly lady would be as hospitable as she'd been on the previous occasion, as tea and a slice of cake would be a welcome addition to their expedition. The front door to the building was open, and they made their way up the stairs to the apartment. The door to Madame Thibeaux's apartment was also open, but there were no signs of movement. No maid rushed about with washing or groceries, in too great a hurry to concern herself with anything as trivial as closing the door.

'Madame Thibeaux?' Mary called out.

That was no response. Not even the parrot, Monsieur Francis, who had previously been gracious with his greetings, squawked a welcome.

'This is most peculiar.' Mary turned to Jane, her brow furrowed.

Something in the silence made her feel uneasy. Tentatively, she stepped into the open doorway, making her way slowly towards the sitting room with the panoramic window. Mary made no sound; if there was something or someone else here, she did not want to draw attention to herself.

'Madame Thibeaux?' she called again, her voice scarcely more than a whisper. 'Madame… Oh!' Mary froze; the words caught in her throat at the sight before her. The door to the golden birdcage was wide open, and the body of Madame Thibeaux was lying face-down in a pool of blood.

'Oh no!' Mary rushed to the old lady, taking Madame Thibeaux's wrist in her fingers, desperate to find a sign of life. There was no pulse, and the red pool on the floor was matched by a wound that glistened against her shock of white hair like a ruby amongst snow.

'Monsieur Francis?' Jane stammered. 'I wonder where he is…'

Mary looked at her quizzically. There was a dead body in front of them, and Jane's primary concern was for the parrot. It must be the shock. They could only hope he'd had the good sense to fly away.

'This has happened recently.' Mary knelt, squinting at the back of Madame Thibeaux's head. 'The blood has not yet congealed around the wound…'

'We must contact the gendarmes,' Jane said, turning away with distaste. 'If we are seen with the body, we will become the chief suspects.' Jane started to pace around the room. 'But if we go to the gendarmes, are we not the only suspects?' Jane continued, panicking. 'Mary, we cannot go to the gendarmes. We must leave, now.'

'I didn't see anyone on our way into the building,' Mary said. 'Did you?'

Jane shook her head, then asked, 'Did Madame Thibeaux have a housekeeper?'

'Yes, she did. Why?'

'Then where is she?'

'Well, today is Wednesday, is it not? Market day in Paris.' Mary frowned at a sudden thought. Had not Claudine Lamont's disappearance also been on a market day? And the woman they had seen in Troyes who bore a resemblance to Madame Lamont — had *that* been a market day?

'Is it not strange that Madame Lamont's disappearance and Madame Thibeaux's death both occurred on a market day?' Mary said, thinking aloud. 'The only day of the week on which the servants would be absent, leaving the woman of the house home alone.'

'The sun is high; the street outside will be busier.' Jane nodded towards the front door to the apartment. She was right. It was only a matter of time before someone came into the building, and the last thing they needed was to be found with the body. Mercifully, Madame Thibeaux's was the only apartment at the top, which meant there would be no immediate intrusion.

'You are right. We must go to the station. But first, there is something else we must do…'

Jane kept watch at the front of the apartment while Mary searched for any clue as to why Madame Thibeaux had called them back. Her previous information about Madame Lamont had been helpful in taking their search to Troyes; perhaps she'd thought of somewhere else they might try. When they'd seen her last, Mary had got the feeling that the old lady knew more than she was letting on. Perhaps there was something she hadn't trusted them with and — if that was the case — what had changed? Mary opened the wardrobe in Madame Thibeaux's bedroom with a heavy heart, her hands trembling as she rifled through her clothing, items she might have loved and now would never wear again. The bedside drawers yielded nothing. Defeated, she walked back into the sitting room.

'Nothing?' Jane whispered.

'Nothing,' Mary replied.

Her gaze swept the sitting room. There had been no clues in the bedroom, and Mary couldn't imagine that any clues would be found in the bathroom or kitchen, so this room was their last hope. She tapped her finger against her lips as she walked around.

'What did you talk of, when you were here with Percy?' Jane asked.

'Let me see … we talked of Madame Lamont's kindness, and her love of painting, reading, and flowers. Madame Thibeaux herself is — was — an educated, worldly woman with a revolutionary zeal.'

'She sounds, if I may say, like your mother, Mary.'

Jane's words were well-intentioned, but they landed on Mary like a blow, reminding her that another link to her mother had been severed.

'Yes, I imagine my mother to have been composed of such fire…' She looked around the room. Madame Thibeaux's political leanings clearly did not prevent her from living a life of opulence. Mary's eyes fell on the table at the back of the room. The last time she and Percy had been here, the table had been empty, but now there was a statue of a woman on top of it.

'Jane, look at this.'

Mary inspected the table. The golden figure was clearly very expensive, and it shone with the haughty bearing of beauty.

'Who is it?' Jane asked.

'Athena. Goddess of wisdom and war.'

'What's that next to it?'

Mary straightened. She'd been so preoccupied with the statue that she hadn't noticed the surrounding items. Now she gave her full attention to them. She saw there was a book and a playbill next to the statue. Mary picked up the playbill.

'It is the programme for *La Comédie Française* on Wednesday the thirteenth of July. That was the date Madame Lamont was supposed to meet her husband at the Théâtre Montansier.'

'So, Madame Thibeaux was there too?' Jane queried.

Mary nodded slowly. 'But if she was there, and she knew that Madame Lamont was not, why didn't she say so?'

Jane shrugged. Mary tried to consider what had led Madame Thibeaux to conceal this fact. Her mind was blank. Instead, she picked up the brown leather book and gasped.

'It is my mother's book. Her *Letters Written in Sweden, Norway and Denmark.*'

Mary leafed through the book, hoping for some annotation or veiled message. Madame Thibeaux had clearly expected their visit and had laid these items out in readiness. Perhaps whoever had killed her had wanted to prevent her from talking to Mary and had not seen the seemingly random objects on the table as offering up any sort of clue.

'Is there … anything?' Jane asked.

Mary shook her head. 'No.' She reached the end of the book. On the penultimate page was a dedication written in Latin: *Cum affectione*, Casimir Fleetwood. Though her Latin was rusty, Mary was able to translate it.

'"With affection, Casimir Fleetwood". That's odd.'

'How so?' Jane asked.

'Casimir is the titular character in my father's novel, *Fleetwood.*'

'I must confess I have not read it,' Jane said. 'Tell me, what happens in it?'

'It is the story of a man who travels…' Mary held the book in her hand, rotating it thoughtfully. 'But he does not travel to any of the places my mother writes about… He travels to Switzerland.'

'Switzerland?'

'Perhaps it is a clue. Perhaps in the time we have been in Troyes, Madame Thibeaux heard from Madame Lamont and knew her to be in Switzerland. Perhaps Madame Lamont does not want Monsieur Lamont to know that she is there.'

'But are we not duty-bound to tell Monsieur Lamont of all we know?'

'We are duty-bound to uncover the truth, Jane,' Mary corrected.

CHAPTER FOURTEEN

Percy was starting to think it was something he'd said — it was either that or the musty smell of his attire, which had worsened over the course of his journeys. The woman with the resemblance to Madame Lamont — Pascale — had disappeared again. No sooner had he turned around at the market than she'd disappeared into the crowd, nowhere to be seen. He and Napoleon had made their lonely way to the last row of bankers to secure more funds.

Success was found at the last one, a noble business under the name Marr, Lavigne and Dupont. It was Monsieur Lavigne that Percy had spoken to, and the man's love of the poetic works of Lord Byron and his awareness of *Queen Mab* had secured Percy an additional advance of eighty Napoleons — more than enough to secure decent rooms, meals, and passage back home to England. Percy was tired of adventure and had come to the realisation that he was just putting off the inevitable. Harriet was pregnant with his second child, and he had already received letters telling him they were the scandal of London society, with rumours swirling around that he had started a hedonistic cult and was in a relationship with both sisters.

He had long regretted the decision to allow Jane to join them, but what real choice had they had? She had held all the cards with her knowledge of their elopement and sly indications that she had read every one of the letters that she passed between him and Mary. If he hadn't allowed her to join them, she would have surely informed William Godwin and ruined her own sister's name in society, causing her to fall further than she had already through her association with him. Mary Jane had made it abundantly clear that Percy and Mary shouldered all the responsibility — and blame — for this situation. Jane was nothing more than an innocent girl who had been swept along with the idea of adventure.

Innocent. He laughed to himself. If only Mary Jane knew. If she had seen how Jane had lowered her nightgown when she'd called him to her room under the pretence of a fear of cockroaches, she would not call her innocent. It had taken an iron will to refuse her advances and then many hours more to console her. She had pleaded with him not to tell Mary, not wanting to make public her awkward attempts to share in Mary's romance. It was an odd type of flattery, he supposed, that she should idolise Mary so much that she should desire to emulate her relationship. It was less flattering for himself; Mary was the revered object, not him. Perhaps going back to London and delivering Jane back to her parents would give him and Mary the freedom to love as they wanted to.

Percy booked his tickets on the package coach back to Paris; so much for Monsieur Lamont's claim that no such transportation was possible. His ankle was much improved, but still not up to the task of three long days of arduous walking. Besides, he had arranged to meet Mary by the wooden Arc de Triomphe at the end of the Champs-Élysées. They had agreed that Mary and Jane would make their way there each day at midday and one day, one joyous day, they would finally be reunited. But it would not be today. Percy needed to pack up their things and ensure transportation of them.

The hoteliers had offered Napoleon a home; this was not ideal, but it was preferable to a market in which he would meet an uncertain end. This way, they would know he was being looked after, with a field to roam in and grass to graze. When he came to say goodbye to Napoleon, there was an unexpected lump in his throat and a heaviness in his heart that he had not anticipated.

'*À bientôt*, Napoleon,' he said fondly.

The donkey brayed in response, nuzzling Percy's neck.

Walking away brought back memories of leaving his daughter, Ianthe. He recalled the sunlight dancing on her brown curls, her soft laughter carried on the breeze. He wondered how she would look now; not so much time had passed to make her unrecognisable. A dark thought came, chilling him to the marrow — what if he never saw her again? It would be no less than he deserved, having deserted her mother and brought shame upon the family, but he hoped she resembled him in sensibilities. If she did, she would grow to see the importance of following one's heart, wherever it should lead.

The love he had felt for Harriet had been nothing compared to the grand passion between himself and Mary. Mary was his soulmate; he had felt it immediately, the second her gaze met his at Godwin's dinner table on that chilly evening in March, where the flames of the candles had ignited something deeper within him. Her eyes had such soulfulness that he'd found himself haunted by them, instantly infatuated with her. Godwin had pontificated on the nature of publishing and the great expenses of business, but Percy had found his gaze returning to his enigmatic daughter who he'd been desperate to meet. At last, she was opposite him at the dining table, a young woman possessed of a quiet confidence and charm as warming as the broth he'd swirled around the bowl, not wanting to tell his host that the thought of eating meat made him sick to his stomach. A great weight seemed to anchor him to her; he'd never felt a love that carried such expectation before.

If only life could be all love and nothing else — no responsibility, concern or money. Their life together had been encumbered by more than it should have. Now they had money and did not need to depend on Monsieur Lamont. They could pay back the money he had advanced and return to England, and he and Mary could move away from London and the judgements of society. So long as they were together, it did not matter to him where they went.

'Switzerland?' Jane shouted. 'We must go to Switzerland?'

'You do not need to accompany us. We can send word back to your mother, and I'm sure she will take the next packet steamer over to collect you. Or perhaps you have already sent word and we can expect her to land before we do?'

'Now you are just being foolish, Mary.'

'I apologise, Jane. I am out of sorts. This heat is very disagreeable to me. We do not have heat like this in London. I should have perished years ago if we had.'

'If we were the sort of refined young women to carry fans and reticules, we would not have these issues.'

'A hand fan would be no opponent to the sun, Jane, no matter how hardy.' Mary sighed and sat down on a bench on the promenade. At least it was nice to look over the River Seine, to watch the rowing boats glide along in their slow rhythm, oars hitting the water like outstretched hands. 'Let us go to the river's edge and hire a boat. It may help us cool down and consider our next steps.'

Without waiting for a reply, Mary stood up and walked across to where weathered seamen were hiring out the boats.

'I would like to hire a boat, please,' she said.

One of the men looked up at her, his wizened face half-hidden under his black hat. 'Have you steered a boat before?'

'Many times,' she lied. It was only a small lie. She had been in rowing boats and had watched them, quite mesmerised, as they'd sailed up and down the Thames.

'Very well,' he replied, pointing to the sign outlaying the cost of their adventure. Mary handed over the money.

'Jane, come along.'

Jane followed slowly, looking about her as if fearing that someone she knew might see her. Mary harboured no such concerns, stepping onto the boat with a confidence the boat did not share; it wobbled uncertainly as she manoeuvred herself into position at the back, ushering Jane towards the opposite end.

'I shall oversee steering; you shall oversee direction,' Mary said, firmly.

The colour drained from Jane's cheeks and she nodded, wordless except for an audible gulp. *It will do her good to concentrate on a task*, Mary thought. She also wanted a chance to reorder her own mind.

'Let us row out to that bridge, then back again. We can discuss the case as we go.' Mary bit her lip. She didn't even know which way to hold the oars or which direction they should go in. She looked around; other people seemed to be rowing in an anticlockwise direction; she would do the same.

The boatman was watching them with interest. He waited until they were safely positioned in the boat, then freed it from its mooring and pushed it out into the water. It wobbled again and Mary's stomach lurched with it, but she breathed deeply and rowed, enjoying the gentle heat on her arms as they pushed against the water. From this position, the sun was tempered by the coolness of the water and the gentle breeze across it. For the first time in weeks, Mary felt refreshed. Her mind instantly cleared.

'Here is my latest theory, Jane,' she began. 'I think Madame Thibeaux knew all along that Madame Lamont meant to leave her husband and that she meant to go to Switzerland to start a new life.'

'Right,' Jane replied, looking a little doubtful.

Mary pulled the boat in that direction. Jane lurched forward.

'No, no, I did not mean right as in direction, more as in "go on…"'

'Oh, my mistake.' Mary evened the boat up. 'Anyway, knowing that Monsieur Lamont had commissioned our investigations, Madame Thibeaux knew she had to be careful about what she said, so it is highly possible that she sent us on a fool's errand to Troyes to allow Madame Lamont more time to escape to Switzerland.'

'I suppose it is possible,' Jane agreed. 'If they were such good friends, as you say.'

'Well, we only have Marie and Madame Thibeaux's word for that, and not even Madame Thibeaux's anymore.'

'But who would want to kill Madame Thibeaux?' Jane asked. 'Steer left; there's another boat to the right.'

'Someone who does not wish us to follow Madame Lamont.' Mary turned to look over her shoulder, pulling on the oars as she did so. The gentle heat in her muscles had quickly turned to flame. This was requiring a much greater effort than she had expected.

'Left, left!' Jane shouted.

'I am trying…' Mary replied, gritting her teeth and pushing on, though her muscles felt stretched to snapping point. That sense of calm she'd felt moments earlier had been eclipsed by panic. 'Perhaps if you take an oar and steer towards you, that will…'

Mary let go of the oar. Jane snapped forward to grab it, but it sank below the surface before she could. It bobbed back up in the water several feet beyond the boat, completely out of reach.

They sat back in the boat.

'What do we do?' Mary asked.

'Steer towards the other oar, then when we are close enough, I can stretch out a hand to grab it. It keeps bobbing up in the water over there, see?' She pointed towards the water. Mary noted the direction in which Jane was pointing and attempted to steer the boat with one oar towards its lost mate. But the tide was against them, and all Mary's attempts to steer them in one direction did nothing more than steer them further out.

'Oh no, look!' Jane looked behind her.

Mary squinted towards the shoreline to see what Jane was looking at. The boatman was making his way towards them with a bigger boat and an angry expression on his face.

'Quick, let us retrieve the oar before he devours us…' Mary frantically steered towards the oar as the boatman gained on them.

'Nearly there…' Jane's outstretched arm was in the water. 'Steer a little closer, Mary…' The right side of Jane's body skimmed against the surface.

'There. Got it.' Jane flicked the oar back into the boat, bringing with it a gush of water that splashed into Mary's eyes. She closed them for the briefest of moments, long enough to career into the side of the angry boatman's vessel.

'Come along, I think that is enough adventure for you two,' he said crossly, putting a hand on their boat to attach it to his own. Their own boat wobbled perilously, like a child reluctant to hold its parent's hand.

'We are quite capable of getting to shore without assistance.' Mary's voice was steely in the face of unwanted, and unmerited, authority. 'We will make our own way — thank you all the same.'

The sailor looked at Mary. Her fierce gaze met his own and did not back down. He shrugged and sailed back to the shore alone. Mary made no attempt to recommence rowing until he was firmly back on dry land.

'The nerve of that man.' She shook her head. 'He saw two women taking a boat and made the unfounded assumption that we would sooner or later hit trouble. So much for emancipation.'

'Precisely.' Jane shook her head in his direction, then added, 'Although we had lost an oar.'

They both laughed at this and as they steered back towards the edge of the riverbank, Jane resumed their earlier conversation. 'Have you considered that perhaps Madame Lamont is having an affair and is trying to cover her tracks? Perhaps if she does not wish to be found, she will go to any lengths to prevent it.'

'A similar thought had crossed my mind,' Mary agreed. 'But it falls down on one basic point. I cannot believe that a woman would kill another woman, and a friend at that, merely to conceal a love affair.'

'Does love not make people behave in monstrous ways?'

'Women cannot afford to behave in monstrous ways.' Mary rowed with a renewed vigour, the oars thrashing against the water. 'Even if they should wish it, society does not allow it. Society is very quick to blame the woman, however foul the deeds of the man.'

She thought of Percy. How far would he have gone to escape Harriet? Would he have killed to be with Mary? It was highly unlikely — Percy would not even eat meat, so it was inconceivable to think that he would do harm to another human, however high his passions.

'If she has eloped with a man, then perhaps it is he who is keen to sever all ties?'

Mary nodded. 'Yes, I am inclined to believe that is more likely. Perhaps the man has a lot to lose if the elopement is known.'

'Then what kind of man are we talking about?'

They had finally reached the shore. The boatman took off his hat and wiped the sweat from his brow as he watched the rowing boat float towards him. Mary enjoyed the smug sensation that swept over her in such moments of triumph, a fire that no amount of water could extinguish. She felt it keenly and knew it to be the greatest power in the world. The power that made a god of a man and a goddess of a woman — a power that depended on only the self, which was what made it so impenetrable.

'We must be away to our meeting place. I do not imagine that Percy is there already, but we cannot take the risk. Monsieur Lamont will be waiting for an update, and I have questions of my own.' Mary hitched up her skirt, refused the offer of help to get out of the boat, and positioned herself firmly on dry land. Jane followed suit, but she accepted the boatman's hand. Mary could feel his eyes upon them as they walked up the riverbank and down past the intermittent stalls of chestnuts and painters towards the Champs-Élysées. Paris was slowly finding its feet after the years of war and uncertainty. Mary felt she was doing the same.

CHAPTER FIFTEEN

Percy had spent a quiet afternoon in the field next to the hotel, reading Greek mythology to an unappreciative Napoleon. Having agreed to leave Napoleon behind with hoteliers, he was determined to spend his last afternoon in Troyes with the donkey before joining the coach to Paris. His luggage had already departed and, with a good speed, he would find himself there by nightfall tomorrow.

It was impossible to know where Mary and Jane had taken rooms, though lack of finances would prevent them from returning to the hotel in Marais. He thought that they would have taken rooms near the theatres, hopefully finding somewhere at least safe and warm, if no better than that. This adventure had proved to him he could live a very basic life if needed. The grandiosity of his title — the incoming 3rd Baronet of Castle Goring, Sussex — was nothing compared to the peace of mind he felt from living on his own terms. Peacefulness turned into sleep, and he awoke to find a bee buzzing around his head, a pillow and mattress comprising grass and daisies.

He took out his journal, listened to the sounds of nature that engulfed his senses, and dove into the smells of the world around him like a bee dives into a flower.

If I were to lie in any place from home
Then let this soil envelop me in hand
Then let these bees weave garments spun with gold
Wrap me into eternity in this land.

He scratched it out. No. It wouldn't do. Percy put his hand to his forehead, and a ladybird jumped onto his quill. He twirled it in the late afternoon sun, impressed by the little beetle's tenacity, by its stubborn determination to hold on. It was a chant he had recited to himself many times during his twenty-two years.

'Nothing? You have uncovered nothing?' Monsieur Lamont stared at Mary and smacked his desk with a fist. 'What have I been paying you for?'

'To investigate your wife's disappearance,' Mary replied plainly. 'I take it that she has not reappeared?'

'No, of course not.' He huffed loudly.

'Then we shall continue to investigate. Perhaps we could talk to the cook today, if she is at home.'

'Yes, she should be at home today,' he said, staring into space as if trying to pluck his home schedule out of the air.

'And we may speak to her?'

'She is not one for polite conversation and you may find her a little abrasive, but yes, you may speak to her.'

'You have received no word from your wife?' Mary ventured.

'No, nothing.' He sighed. 'Did you speak to any of her acquaintances?'

'We spoke to Madame Thibeaux — she led us to Troyes, as you know.'

'And you found nothing there?'

'We did at first find someone matching Madame Lamont's description…' Mary started, smoothing down the folds of her skirt as she spoke. 'But upon speaking to her, it became clear that she was not your wife.'

'Did you not think to bring her back with you? What if it *had* been Claudine, but she outsmarted you with a ready lie?'

For the first time, desperation and panic appeared on Monsieur Lamont's features.

'Even if she does not want to come back to me, I need to know that she is safe,' he continued. 'Anything else we can … we can work on; her wellbeing is my only concern.'

'And ours, Monsieur Lamont, but as we told you in our first interview, we are not investigators, but writers, travellers and thinkers.'

'And yet you were quick enough to take my money.' He folded his arms. 'That means you must find my wife, and I expect you to find her quickly. There has been enough messing about.'

'As soon as we have any information, we shall return.'

'You do not need to talk to me in person. We have a postal system here. You may use it. I expect *regular* communication.' He raised his voice to emphasise his demand.

'Then *regular* communication you shall have. Good day to you, Monsieur Lamont.'

Once outside the building, Mary breathed out deeply, her hands shaking.

'What happened in there?' Jane asked. 'Did you tell him about Madame Thibeaux?'

Mary narrowed her eyes. 'That is not the question you should ask, Jane. The more pertinent question is, why didn't he tell me about her?'

'I don't understand…' Jane looked confused.

'Let me explain. Monsieur Lamont acted as though we had missed our chance to bring Madame Lamont back from Troyes. We know that he knew Madame Thibeaux told us of that link, because we told him that.'

Jane frowned. 'No, I still do not follow…'

'What if, having known that we were going to Troyes, he in fact planted his wife there? Did it not seem incredible that the woman in Troyes should tell us so frankly that others had commented on the likeness? What if there were no likeness at all? We have no proof that the likeness Madame Thibeaux gave us was Madame Lamont and no way of questioning her now.'

Their night at the hotel was restless. Mary had pushed their luggage up against the door to prevent any unwanted nocturnal visitors from entering their room, and Jane was worried about visitors of the six-legged kind. Either way, sleep proved an elusive mistress, and the lantern remained lit until the first glimmers of daylight peeped through the shuttered window.

Mary's dreams, when they had eventually come, had comprised dark spaces, the same half-known but unrecognisable landscape that had plagued her nights with increased frequency since they'd started their adventure. In the moments before dawn, she identified it as guilt, her conscience's way of processing that sentiment towards Harriet that she tried her best to ignore, but which sometimes gnawed away at her. By the time the sun had risen, those sentiments had moved out of focus, and she hoped that today would be the day they would meet Percy at the Arc de Triomphe and make their way out of Paris.

Breakfast was taken in the Tuileries, the determined greenery being the perfect accompaniment to their pastries and apples. Conversation was stilted and awkward; Jane, without sleep, was not the most sociable of creatures and Mary enjoyed the opportunity to sit and watch the gentle Parisians promenading around the park. Here there were no ravages of battle, no outward signs of the scars that the countryside had worn, just the natural world continuing as it had before the conflict and as it would doubtless carry on long after its inhabitants had gone. Jane turned her face up to the sunshine, closing her eyes.

'This is a beautiful place, is it not? I think I could live here.'

Mary rolled her eyes. Oh, to be as naïve as Jane and to love and want to stay everywhere. For Mary, it was even simpler than that; her heart wanted to be wherever Percy was.

'Living in the park is about all our finances would stretch to in the long term,' Mary replied.

'Do you suppose Percy has secured funds?' Jane turned to look at her sister, squinting in the sunlight.

'We shall know soon enough.' Mary stretched out on the grass. 'I hope so.'

'Perhaps one day I shall take rooms in Paris and become an actress on the stage. Do you think that is likely?' Jane asked with a smile.

'There is a look of Aphra Behn about you. I think it is no more or less likely than any other plan,' Mary answered. When Jane huffed, Mary attempted to backtrack. 'What I mean to say is that if you have a mind to do it and the talent to do it, then I cannot see that you would let any obstacle stand in your way.' Jane rolled onto her front and kicked her legs up in the air. 'Do you think me so very determined, Mary? Do you think I will always get what I want?'

Mary knew she meant Percy, but she determined that nothing and no one was going to dampen her spirits today.

'We are to see Monsieur Lamont's cook this morning, are we not?' Jane sat up, brushing the grass off her skirts. Mary was glad about the change in conversation.

'We are. Shall we away now?'

Without waiting for a response, Mary got up from the lawn and walked towards the entrance to the public garden. The church bells chimed nine. It was still early; with any luck, they would have time enough to visit the cook and still be in time to meet Percy. Something told her that today would be the day he arrived. There was an extra energy fizzing up inside her, the sort she only got when he was near. Mary bit her lip, a sudden apprehensiveness clouding her thoughts — she would have to tell him about Madame Thibeaux and the trip to Switzerland. What if he didn't want to go and thought her actions nothing but an impulsive fool's errand? She would have to convince him of the efficacy of her plan; the only trouble was that she hadn't quite convinced herself.

Mercifully, the morning was devoid of the stifling heat that had pervaded their earlier walks around Paris, and the gentle summer breeze made the walk to Monsieur Lamont's house infinitely more pleasant than their reception upon arrival. Far from being greeted by the pleasant and cooperative Marie, it was the gardener Patrice who opened the door with a glower.

'Back again?' he growled.

'We are here to see the cook; I believe Monsieur Lamont has arranged it for us?'

Patrice pulled the door open, walking them through to the kitchen in silence.

'Delphine, it's Madame Shelley. Lamont's sent her.'

The cook had her back turned to them; she was pounding her fists into a mixture of dough, pulling and stretching it into submission. When she turned to greet them, the dough moved with her.

'I'm very busy,' she said through gritted teeth, turning back to her pummelling.

'We will not keep you long.' Mary tried to sound respectful and firm, holding her hands together politely. She coughed lightly to keep a nervous tremor from her voice. 'We just have a few questions about Madame Lamont.'

'She has been missing for almost a month. A month!' The cook twisted the dough into a long, thin line, then pulled it apart. 'I think a man's involved — there's always a man involved.'

She turned to the gardener, who looked down, clearly as unwilling to meet her gaze as Mary and Jane were. That was a first — someone grumpier than he was.

'I will be outside with the roses…' He scuttled away.

'Always a man involved,' Delphine repeated, tutting to herself. Mary watched as she put the twisted dough onto a tray and cast it into the open fire of the oven. The task completed, she brushed the flour from her hands and then wiped them down the front of her apron.

'Right, that has got him out of the way. What do you want to know?'

Mary was taken aback by the cook's sudden change of disposition.

'Monsieur Lamont has charged us with finding information about his wife's disappearance. What can you tell us about her?' she managed.

Delphine sniffed, rolling her shoulders. 'She had no more to do with the staff than she had to, do you know what I mean? For all her pretty speeches about rights and freedom, she wasn't so concerned with workers' rights within the home.'

'She wasn't a kind mistress?' Jane asked.

'No, I didn't say that, did I? Only that she wasn't the sort of mistress to make friends with, let's put it that way. She had her things to do, and I had mine.'

147

'Have you any idea where she might have gone, or why she might have left?'

'Monsieur Lamont's always tied up with some deal or other; perhaps she got bored with being alone. Rich people often go missing because they want to; poor people who go missing are probably dead.'

Mary inhaled sharply.

The cook looked at her, shrugged, and carried on with her tasks. 'Look, if you're asking if she was unhappy, I would say no, not that I could see. If you're asking if Monsieur Lamont was a monster, I would say no more than any other man. What do I think happened? I do not know; I keep myself to myself.'

Delphine mumbled some other words under her breath; Mary didn't catch them. Whatever tolerance she'd felt towards Mary and Jane was reaching its natural end.

'Can I ask you one more question?' Mary asked tentatively.

The cook sighed. 'If it will mean that you go away and let me get on with my work, then yes, please do.'

'Have you been to the market in Troyes in the past two weeks?'

'Troyes? Why would I go to the market there when there are markets enough in Paris?'

Mary and Jane soon found themselves back on the driveway, no further ahead now they'd seen the cook. A snipping of shears warned Mary that the gardener was watching their every move. She linked arms with Jane to hasten her along — the sooner they were away from him, the better. It was a shame Marie the housemaid hadn't been in; she had been so much easier to talk to than Delphine, lacking her weariness and natural suspicion.

Whilst they had been indoors, the sun had come out and now loomed in the sky like a brilliant orange ball. Heat bounced off the trees and once again Mary cursed her sartorial decisions. Wearing all black had seemed like a sophisticated thing to do when packing her trunk, but she had not taken continental climates into consideration at all, thinking only of the pale skies of London, whose indistinguishable drizzle offered no clues as to the season. The sudden thought of London cast a shadow on her spirits, dragging them down as she and Jane made their way towards the meeting point. Despite her letters to her father, there had been no word in return, no sign of the slightest thaw in his feelings towards her. It was almost too much to bear to think they might be estranged forever; escaping from London had been a tremendous adventure, but it could become a curse if they had to keep plodding from place to place, scrapping for money and shelter. There was no conceivable way they could carry on like this for much longer. But without a home or family, it was hard to see what they would go back for.

The midday sun was at its highest as they reached the Arc de Triomphe. Mary kept her eyes on the road, excitement bubbling in her veins, giving her a nervous energy that made her want to jump around like a hot cricket. Jane kept watch in the other direction, her gaze more focused and her body still.

'Oh look, he's here, he's here!' Mary jumped up and down. A well-dressed couple delivered sharp, disapproving tuts as they walked past her.

The coach pulled up by the side of the road, the horses that pulled it shaking sweat from their manes, which landed on the driver. The man muttered expletives with wide-armed gestures in response. Percy did not see Mary at first, his gaze falling towards the sweating horses, smiling at their militancy. When his gaze fell upon her, it was as if there was another sun shining on her, evaporating every doubt and ill thought she had harboured. Mary rushed to him. He swept her up in his arms and they kissed without a care for the attention they were garnering from the passers-by.

'Thank goodness you are back.' Mary wrapped her arms around his neck, her soul at peace even though her heart raced.

'I am as overjoyed at our reunion as you are.'

Percy motioned for the driver to leave his luggage at the side of the road, then beckoned to Jane.

'Jane, could you give me a hand with this? You are admirably strong, and I must have a moment with Mary.'

Jane turned to drag the trunk, her murderous expression unnoticed by Percy.

'How did it go with Madame Thibeaux?'

'Hideous,' Mary whispered. 'She was murdered.'

'Murdered?' Percy gasped, his volume making the horses turn their heads. 'How?'

'She had been hit on the back of her head. There was a lot of blood…'

'Is there a link here? A disappearance, then a murder? What if you're next, Mary? Do you suppose that whoever came for Madame Thibeaux may come for you? Perhaps someone is desperate for Madame Lamont to stay hidden.' He swallowed, his eyes suddenly wide with alarm.

'I had similar fears,' Mary confided, 'and fears that whoever committed such a terrible deed did so with the express purpose of framing me.'

'Framing you?'

'The telegram at the hotel?' Mary reminded him. 'Is it not too much of a coincidence that we turn up at Madame Thibeaux's apartment to find her newly killed?'

'But who could have known such a thing?' Jane interrupted from behind them. 'Not even Monsieur Lamont would have known we were on our way back to Paris or the time it would take to get back. Unless...'

'Unless he sent the telegram?' Mary suggested.

'I saw the woman in Troyes again,' Percy added. 'She was at the market. She told me that the cook had told her of her likeness to Madame Lamont.'

'The cook?' The thud from behind them made Mary and Percy jump. Jane had dropped the trunk.

'What is it?' Percy looked at Jane, and then at Mary, a quizzical look on his face.

'We saw the Lamonts' cook this morning, and she is adamant that she does not visit the market in Troyes,' said Mary.

'But if it was not the cook, then who approached the woman?'

'We shall endeavour to find out, but first let us deposit your luggage into our room. I have booked a second room for Jane, now you have returned.'

Jane huffed, picked up the trunk, and trundled behind them.

'Do not expect luxury; it is barely a blanket on a hard slab of hay.'

'But I shall sleep with you, my dearest. That will make it as comfortable as a cloud.'

They made their way to the hotel, ignoring the sly grin of the hotelier, who smacked his lips and snickered when Mary called Percy her husband. When he spied the room, Percy's face was a noble study of a man trying, but failing, to hide his disappointment.

Mary shrugged. 'I told you it was basic.'

'Is that a…' Percy pointed towards the ground, where an insect rushed past.

'Probably, but the rooms are cheap and reasonably comfortable. Not entirely what you might call safe, but safer now we have your trunk to perch against the door.'

'We have money now, Mary. Surely we can use some of it to secure better accommodation?'

'Let us use it for the next leg of our adventure…' Mary's eyes shone. 'For we are Switzerland-bound.'

CHAPTER SIXTEEN

There was one more task to complete before they left Paris — a visit to the Théâtre Montansier. Mary and Jane would try to talk to the actors whilst Percy sorted the transportation to Switzerland. One night in that hotel was enough to convince him of the efficacy of private, comfortable travel arrangements. Mary had watched as he'd stroked the straw in his sleep, claiming it reminded him of the time he'd fallen asleep next to Napoleon on a sunny day in Troyes. His nostalgic mood had not lasted the night, and he'd woken with a cricked neck and a constant yawn. Still, the cool, bright morning and the host of flowers that seemed to have sprung up outside the hotel overnight were enough to brighten anyone's mood, Mary reasoned.

Unfortunately, it wasn't enough to brighten Jane's mood, and she spent the entire walk to the theatre rubbing at her shoulder. 'Percy can transport his own trunk next time,' she hissed.

The theatre's exterior shone like a white sandcastle against the cobbled street. It was hard to believe that it was only a stone's throw from those criminal pockets where shady figures appeared out of the shadows and disappeared back into them at the same speed. Mary was surprised that Paris, just like London, could house the very highest and lowest of society as neighbours. The alternating streets had brought with them conflicting commentary from Jane — she'd marvelled at the cleanliness of the cobbles and the lightness of the air in one, before turning a corner and bemoaning the choking, glutinous air and lifeless, grey buildings of another.

An exclamation from a window was followed by a splash of water. Mary and Jane jumped back, and held their noses at the sights and sounds that assailed their senses. A door opened, this one belonging to the theatre, and an angry man held up a fist to the window. His hot words were met with insults and gestures of equal heat. Mary saw her chance.

'Good morning, my name is Mary God... Mary Shelley, and this is my sister Jane. May we trouble you for a couple of minutes of your time?'

The man shook a handkerchief out of his pocket, put it first to his forehead then to his nose, nodded and gestured them inside. They took seats at a dimly lit table, where Mary unrolled the playbill found at Madame Thibeaux's apartment from her pocket and showed it to the man, who introduced himself as the theatre's manager.

'Can you tell me how long has this play been in performance?'

'*La Comédie Française* is the highlight of our summer season; it has been playing since June.'

'Do you keep records of patrons? Sales?'

'We keep records of sales, yes, and we are fortunate to have several very special patrons.'

'Would you be able to tell us if Monsieur Lamont, the banker near Rue d'Anjou, had been in attendance this season?'

'Monsieur and Madame Lamont are two of our most loyal patrons.'

'And they have seen this play?' Mary pointed to the playbill.

'As patrons, they will have received complimentary tickets. I believe they attended the opening night and enjoyed it so much they booked again.'

'And did they attend again?'

The theatre manager shrugged. 'I pay little attention once the curtain goes down; perhaps the ticket collector might assist you further.'

'Where might we find him?'

'The theatre is closed this evening, so the tavern with the rest of the company would be my guess. Bar de L'antrac.'

'Thank you.' Mary slid the playbill back into her pocket. 'One final question, if I may. Does the ticket collector have a name?'

'He does, but you must discover that for yourself. I will tell you one thing: he is also known as Sebastien.'

'Well, that is easy; he has two names for two distinct personalities — one in the theatre and one in his everyday life.' That was Percy's response to the theatre manager's puzzle.

'Perhaps he too is an investigator and has a professional name, so his enemies do not find him.' Jane giggled, her cheeks flushed with claret. This was the first time she had ever been to a tavern, and Mary hoped it would not go to her head.

'I feel that there is a much more sensible explanation that we have discarded,' Mary said, turning her gaze to the door every time a sudden breeze alerted her to the entry of a new patron. 'Though what it could be currently eludes me.'

'Perhaps this is Sebastien?' Jane's mouth slackened, and she gave such a deep, pronounced sigh that Mary's curiosity was piqued. A tall man wearing a red military coat and trousers flamed into the building. All chatter stopped; all eyes watched as he strode towards the huddle of people nestled at the back of the tavern. Percy looked down at his own coat and attempted to brush the dirt off it.

'He fancies himself to be something of a peacock, does he not?' Percy folded his arms.

Mary grinned. 'He certainly is most demonstrative of his perceived graces. We prefer more subtlety, don't we, Percy?'

'Quite right, quite right.' Percy nodded, missing the irony and returning to his drink with a reassured smile.

'Does he not have a look of Byron about him?' Jane whispered to Mary.

Jane's eyes had a faraway look. Byron had been her romantic ideal since she'd read *Childe Harold* several years earlier.

'You are right. He does.' Mary nodded enthusiastically, gulping her wine. 'We should talk to him. I feel certain he knows something.' She turned to Percy. 'Percy, Jane has a feeling that the peacock might be the man we are looking for.'

Percy nodded and stretched out on the bench, which groaned beneath him. 'Feel free to make enquiries. I will rest here awhile; I am fatigued from my journey and endeavours.'

Jane darted up, nodding towards the peacock. 'Come along then, Mary.'

It was bad enough to be in a tavern, but it was unheard of for respectable ladies to purposefully walk up to a group of men and make introductions. In England, such behaviour would get a lady marked as a woman of the night. In this particular Parisian tavern, however, no one batted an eyelid and their arrival at the table made no dent in the celebrations enjoyed by the men. The group laughed raucously at something one of them had said, and the collective banging of fists on the table that accompanied their merriment made the table and Mary shake. Jane cleared her throat, but the laughter carried on around them.

'Excuse me, would one of you gentlemen go by the name Sebastien?' she asked in her most fluent French.

'Sebastien?' they roared back at her, shaking their heads and resuming their laughter.

Mary breathed deeply and straightened her spine before she spoke. 'Listen, this is no laughing matter. There is a missing woman and a second woman whose murder may be connected to the first. I suggest you take this question a little more seriously if you do not wish to elevate yourselves to the head of the suspect list.'

That did it. The laughter that had rolled through the tavern moments earlier was replaced by silence. Tankards returning to tables and the scuffle of feet underneath turned the group into a gaggle of censured boys.

'Apologies, we meant no disrespect,' said an older man with a large moustache. 'It is only that *Sebastien* is a term we use for anyone who is … how do you say … engaging in a romantic relationship with a patron of the arts. It is an old term, well known and used by everyone…'

'That is why we laughed; it is a surprise to hear the term used outside the theatre. Where did you hear it?' the peacock asked.

'From the theatre manager,' Mary replied.

'I may offer help.' The peacock got up from the table, moving towards Mary and Jane. He was taller than the lamp posts on Place Furstenberg. 'May I sit with you?'

As they walked towards their table, Mary watched Percy surveying the peacock with a stony, impassive glare. If they'd had feathers, they would both be puffing out their chests and showing their plumage, Mary thought.

'Claret?' Percy offered; the peacock nodded.

'My name is Frederic Martin. I am a playwright with La Commedia Players. *La Comédie Française* is my play.'

'It is very nice to meet you,' Mary said.

'Yes, it is.' Jane coughed, picking up her goblet of claret. She was clearly on her best behaviour.

'Do you know Monsieur and Madame Lamont?' Mary asked. No point in politeness; she was not here to make friends but to solve a mystery.

'Yes, of course, everyone knows them. Monsieur Lamont is a keen patron of the arts; he enjoys spending her money on patronages.'

'Her money?' Percy spluttered.

'Yes, Madame Lamont is from a merchant family. They have great wealth … had great wealth.'

'I am sorry … I am just…' Mary was staggered by her own blindness. She had assumed that the Lamonts' wealthy lifestyle was down to the decisions of Monsieur Lamont, not the inheritance of his wife. 'What do you mean, *had* great wealth?'

'There were rumours of an alliance … some poor, how shall we say, political decisions?'

Having seen the divide between the rich and poor that dominated the Parisian streets, it was easy to believe that even the fronts of extravagant houses could mask crumbling empires within. It was a story that went back to the Roman times; it even applied to her own household. Mary shuddered at the memory of Harriet's wicked rumour that her own father had sold herself and Jane to Percy to pay off his debts — people certainly lost their heads where money was concerned.

'And what about Madame Lamont? Did she make some poor decisions?' Percy asked, staring directly at Frederic.

'If you are asking me if I was having a relationship with Claudine, then the answer is yes, I was. But I have a lot of relationships with patrons; I see it as part of the patronage.' He shrugged. Mary looked at Jane, who sat up straighter now. The playwright continued. 'If you are asking me if I know anything about her disappearance, then the answer is no.'

'Madame Thibeaux knew of your relationship, didn't she?' said Mary.

'Yes, she did.' Frederic sighed, stretching out his leg onto the vacant chair next to him. From the opposite side of the table, Percy did the same. The wooden bench wobbled beneath him, and he put his hand out to steady himself.

'You are Percy Shelley, are you not?' Frederic asked.

'I am.' Percy shot to his feet. 'What of it?'

'I have a copy of *Queen Mab*. I got it in London.'

Percy broke into a wide smile and sat back down in his seat, readjusting his plumage. 'And what did you think of it?'

'I thought some cantos were genius, others less so...'

'Oh, yes? I would be delighted to hear where you feel I could make improvements...' Percy's voice dripped with sarcasm.

'Gentlemen, we can discuss the merits of your poetry and your plays later. For now, we must deal with the issue at hand, the disappearance of Madame Lamont. Tell me, Monsieur Martin, did Monsieur Lamont know of his wife's indiscretion?'

Frederic shook his head. 'No, he did not know. They came to watch the play several times. Claudine, Madame Lamont, came too with her friend, Madame Thibeaux.'

'At whose house you had your assignations?'

'Amongst other places.'

'It sounds like your conduct has been spectacularly indiscreet...' Percy observed.

'What did your great poet William Shakespeare say — love is a child? It takes what it wants, and I take what I want.'

Frederic looked at Jane. It was only a throwaway glance, but Mary knew it was more than enough to fire up Jane's passions.

'How many love affairs do you have per season?' Percy was on a roll now. 'Would you say they were a good promotion for your company?'

'My love-life is no concern of yours; nor is my craft.' Frederic pushed the chair back and stood up. 'Good evening to you all.'

Mary stood quickly. 'I am sorry if Percy's questions have upset you; for a sublime poet, he can be clumsy in his speech,' she said.

Frederic hesitated. Mary glared at Percy, who finally spoke.

'I am sorry if I offended you.'

'Thank you for your apology.' Frederic bowed his head slightly and sat back down. 'Though I fear I have little more to tell you. I do not know where Claudine is. I have not seen her since…'

'Since you made plans to elope to Switzerland? But she did not turn up for the crossing, and it was that which prevented you from being at the play on the night of her disappearance?' Mary spoke firmly.

Frederic's face paled. 'How could you possibly know that?'

CHAPTER SEVENTEEN

As Mary removed her clothes in the hotel room several hours later, she hoped to shed the increasingly heavy burden of Madame Lamont's disappearance along with them. There were so many aspects of the case that made little sense. No one seemed capable of telling them the whole truth, and everyone they had spoken to seemed to shield themselves for their own agenda. Would she ever understand it?

Mary sighed. The nausea had returned with a vengeance, and once she lay down on the bed, the fatigue that she'd carried around all day overwhelmed her. Ever since they'd landed in Paris, it had been one thing after another: the incessant heat, the pressure of the investigation, the recurrent nightmares … and yet the guilt of leaving her father and her sister Fanny behind in London weighed heaviest of all. It felt as though she had severed the ties to her old life and was trying to navigate this new one whilst feeling perpetually adrift. Percy's inability to plan or prepare finance for the trip had been another burden, though one she would have to keep silent on. Still, it was what she had chosen, so she had to make the best of things. In time, perhaps, she could write a travel journal as her mother had done, documenting all these adventures.

'Percy, can I ask you a delicate question? It might be one you are unwilling to answer…'

'If I can answer it, I will.' Percy stopped undoing his boots. 'What is it?'

'My knowledge of affairs of the heart extends only to what I know with you and what I have read. You are more worldly. Would it really be possible to hide a great affection for someone else? Would a husband or wife truly have no inkling at all?'

'I think a husband could — there are fewer opportunities for women to leave the house. It would take a tremendous level of subterfuge to hide an affair for a lady of Madame Lamont's class.'

'But it wouldn't be impossible?'

Percy shook his head. 'No, it wouldn't be impossible.' He smiled at Mary before swooping behind her and taking her in his arms. 'I hope you are not planning any such behaviour... It would crush my soul.'

'I am a fiercely loyal creature, Percy, and once my heart is pierced, it cannot be restored. It is infected with Percy Shelley; your name runs through my veins. How could anyone else compare with that?'

'A most capital answer, Mary, and you are truly the wife of my soul's core. There is nothing but pity for Harriet now; we were young and foolish, and I knew nothing of life or love. Now I know, and have everything.' He kissed her on the cheek. 'Let us away to bed, where our souls can connect in their wordless symphony. Exciting adventures are on the horizon — we can put Paris and this horrible business behind us.'

Mary hugged Percy close. The change of scenery would indeed be welcome, but he was a fool if he did not realise that they would drag all their ghosts along with them.

The letter to Monsieur Lamont was functional and to the point, informing him that all leads regarding his wife in Paris had reached a dead end. Mary wasn't sure what impulse prevented her from telling him about the trip to Switzerland or the revelation of Madame Lamont's lover, but the impulse was real and guiding her like a sole star in a night sky. Their trunks safely packed and sent ahead of their coach to the crossing, Percy attempted to advance more money for the next part of their trip. When he returned several hours later, his pockets were heavier and his step lighter.

'I have another twelve pounds,' he told them, proudly. 'That should see us through the summer.'

Mary smiled but her spirits sank; living from hand to mouth was exhausting. She had even dreamed of her comfortable life at home — even Mary Jane's judgemental looks and unkind words were preferable to this nomadic existence. Funny that the books she had read on the subject, including her mother's words, had all focused on the joys and excitement of travel, the vast superiority of the traveller to the average person, when Mary did not feel in the slightest bit elevated but tired, moody and in need of a good bath. Jane had been invited to a late evening play with Frederic the previous night and she arrived back at the hotel in time for lunch, her tousled hair and dishevelled clothing attracting many whispers and sly looks from the other patrons.

'We were wondering if you would make it back before the coach departs,' Percy said with a laugh.

Mary had half-hoped that she wouldn't. 'I am glad to see you safe and well.'

Jane yawned deeply. 'I am both those things, but I am also in need of a freshen-up.'

'Most of your luggage has been packed away, but I left spare clothes out for such a purpose.'

'Thank you.' Jane smiled.

'Did you have an enjoyable night?' Percy asked with a wink.

'Capital.' Jane's smile grew and her cheeks flushed. 'I will make myself presentable before joining you. I am famished.'

She grabbed a hunk of bread from Mary's plate, nodded her thanks, and walked away.

'With what did he seduce her, I wonder?' Percy whispered to Mary once Jane had left the room. 'Byron, Shakespeare, Molière…'

Mary smiled at him. It was satisfying to see that Percy showed no shred of jealousy regarding Jane's passionate encounter. The diversion away from their own situation seemed to have improved his spirits enormously, for which Mary was very grateful.

'Shall we take a walk around Paris, to bid our *adieus*?' Percy asked.

'I will just tell Jane where we are heading.'

Mary found Jane fast asleep on her bed, the bread still curled in her fist. Rather than wake her up, she left her a note telling her where they had gone and that they would return to collect her at three o'clock that afternoon. That would give her ample time to sleep off the previous evening. Mary and Percy walked out into a calm, early afternoon breeze that made the city refreshing. It was a welcome change from the perpetual heat, which had become as tiresome for Mary as the perpetual rainfall in London.

'Perhaps I should have brought you to a place unravaged by conflict,' Percy said as they walked the sombre streets of the first arrondissement. Conflict had respected the monuments and landmarks but savaged the people; there was no spark in their step, no joy in their hearts. At least in the Latin Quarter, they had alcohol to buoy their spirits. They walked through rows of tall buildings the colour of shortbread, into slices of greenery and cemeteries haunted by the ghosts of the past. After an hour of aimless wandering, they found themselves near Madame Thibeaux's apartment.

The door to the building was open. A couple of children flashed past, brandishing scraps of fabric like weapons and flags. A woman followed not far behind, shouting at them to come back into the house. She stopped and looked at Mary. Mary hesitated. The woman retreated into the house, holding the door open with one hand. The sound of voices from inside the house flew out through open windows. A window in Madame Thibeaux's flat opened. A face peered out, squinting against the glare of the sun.

Now, the woman at the window screamed and pointed at Mary, shouting something that Mary didn't quite catch. She whistled. At the sound of the whistle, a man appeared from a dark doorway opposite the building. Heated words were exchanged between the woman at the window and the man in the doorway, but Mary was rooted to the spot. Her tight throat and quickened pulse told her to run, but something was keeping her in place. The pressure of Percy pulling at her arm brought her back to her senses. The man opposite had shouted for another man, and now there was a mob of angry faces.

'Mary, we need to leave.'

The crowd was gathering in front of the apartment, the two children who'd been the focal point moments earlier now lost in the throng. The grip on Mary's arm tightened.

'Mary, I'm not talking in jest, we need to leave … now!'

Mary blinked, nodded, and allowed Percy to guide her away at a brisk pace. Within seconds, they had quickened their pace to a canter until the building was a memory behind them. Voices mixed and swelled in the air; angry insults and recriminations flew in their direction. Some words Mary caught but did not wish to keep hold of.

'I'm sure someone just shouted for the gendarmes… Do not look back,' Percy said, glancing behind them. They were soon running. The noise of the crowd behind them intensified, thickening the air until Mary could hardly breathe.

'We cannot stop until we've lost them,' Percy went on, through gulps of breath. 'I fear they will lynch us if they get hold of us.'

'What possible reason could they have for wishing us such harm?' Mary panted in reply.

'Don't you see? It is as we feared — someone is framing you for the death of Madame Thibeaux. We are the ones who have been gallivanting round Paris searching for Madame Lamont. We have been everywhere she went; we are the ones who seem desperate to find her. Someone is determined that we will not and will stop at nothing to prevent the discovery of the truth … even murder.'

Percy's proclamation seemed ridiculous, but as Mary turned to look at the crowd, she instantly wished she hadn't: it seemed to have swollen in number. She gulped. Perhaps he was right, but if so, there were few enough people they had met in Paris who knew of their employment with Monsieur Lamont. Mary's lungs burned with the strain, but eventually the roar of the crowd diminished. She looked around; she had absolutely no idea where they were, but so long as they weren't being followed, she didn't much care. Mary breathed deeply, exhaling through her mouth until her lungs were full again.

'The sooner we're out of Paris, the better, wouldn't you say?' said Percy.

'Mind out of the way, would you?'

Bundles of clothes tumbled towards them, a young boy spreadeagled on top. A man swore and the boy was promptly dragged up, wriggling like a fish on a hook.

'There'd better be no dirt on them…'

The hand holding the boy up released him, and he fell back onto the pile of clothes, which he scrambled to pick up. Mary rushed to help him.

'It was our fault; we weren't looking where we were going.' Mary glared at the man and shoved the clothes back into his arms. 'Are you hurt?' she asked the boy. He looked to be only a few years younger than she, his dark clothes worn and dusty. He took off his cap. The curly hair that sprung up was like Percy's.

'No, I fell onto the clothes, so they broke the fall.' He grinned at her, revealing rows of broken teeth.

'Are you related to him?' Mary tipped her head towards the man, who'd taken the clothes and was heading down the road. 'Is that why he thinks he can be so rude to you?'

She'd seen it a million times before, young boys forced into work as soon as they could hold a spade or a chimney brush. Her blood boiled afresh at the thought of it.

'No, Miss, he is not my father. He is my employer; we work for the theatre.'

'The theatre?'

'Yes, Miss, Les Filles et la Sottise.'

'I haven't heard of that. Is it new?'

'No, Miss.' The boy shuffled his feet. 'It is a theatre for gentlemen only.'

'Percy, have you heard of this theatre, the Filles et la Sottise?'

Percy, who'd been keeping one eye behind them lest the mob should reappear, blew out his cheeks. 'So, it exists then. I had heard tales of it in London but thought them to be just that.'

'Have you heard of a playwright called Frederic Martin?' Mary asked the boy.

'I have heard of him, but I haven't met him.'

'How about Madame Lamont — Claudine Lamont?'

The boy shook his head. 'A woman with a name like that would find no amusement in la Sottise.'

'If it isn't too indiscreet —' Percy leant in, casting suspicious glances around — 'will you tell us what sort of people go to this theatre?'

'Well, sir, if I was to be making assumptions about it, I would say fine gentlemen like yourself, professional men — doctors, lawyers, bankers, politicians. They've all been through our doors.'

'Bankers, you say?' Percy cocked his head to the side; it gave him the appearance of a keen terrier. 'Is Pierre Lamont among them?'

'We ask no names and take none, only money; one Sebastien is as good as another.'

'Sebastien?' Mary asked, alert.

'That was the name we gave to them.'

'Was?'

'Our theatre may be for the gentlemen, but the players are women, and trade's fallen off since our star actress upped and left in March.'

An angry whistle flew through the air. The boy's gaze followed it and his face fell. The man who'd taken the bundle of clothes now stood at an open door, gesticulating wildly with arms freed of their former treasures.

'We leave for Troyes tonight. We have new premises there to try.'

Mary found it hard to believe that a sleepy town like Troyes could have such murky depths; it had seemed to her devoid of any passion or spark. Perhaps this theatre was exactly what the townspeople needed.

'One more thing: will the patrons be called Sebastien in Troyes?'

'No, Miss, in Troyes they will be called Thimothé.'

Once the boy departed, Mary scrutinised their surroundings and quickly concluded that she didn't have the first idea how to get back to the hotel. Hoping Percy would have a better notion was foolhardy; his sense of direction was proving to be poor. The tolling of the cathedral bells indicated that they only had one hour in which to make their way back to the hotel, retrieve Jane, and board the coach for the first part of their journey to Switzerland. Fear twisted her stomach: what if the mob came looking for her or, worse, what if they had informed the gendarmes and the entire Parisian police force were following their every move?

She knew that Percy's booking would be in his name only — a private coach needed no more information than the name of the man paying for it, so that wasn't a concern. There would be three of them travelling together, and Mary could only hope that there would indeed be the strength in numbers that people spoke of, but she wasn't about to take any chances. An idea struck her, chiming its good sense as loudly as the cathedral bells.

'Percy, are there any clothing establishments around here?'

Arriving at the coach with only moments to spare, Jane walked with a comical swagger, pulling at her collar.

She tutted. 'I really don't know how men can dress like this; I feel as though I am being suffocated.'

'We men must sacrifice much for the sake of our appearance; you do not realise how lucky you are to be in freeing stays and gowns,' said Percy.

'I am sure we could while away many an hour debating the restrictions of corsets, but I would prefer to get on this coach and make our way out of Paris before I am impounded.' Mary adopted a brisk pace, striding ahead of both Percy and Jane. Unlike Jane, she found the pantaloons they had purchased from the menswear store to be conducive to a hearty pace and a clarity of thought. No wonder they were so popular with poets. A lazy sunset, in no hurry to meld itself with darkness, illuminated their path along the Seine.

Their luggage was attached to the carriage, reminding Mary of the precariously piled hairstyles they'd seen on the smart women of the Champs-Élysées. It had no windows, so there was no chance of enjoying the scenery, but it also minimised the risks of exposure. Once they were out of Paris and any imminent danger, they could travel safely on to Switzerland.

'We leave your mother's footsteps behind, Mary, and step into your father's…' Percy breathed in deeply, as if he were trying to inhale as much of Paris as she was trying to exhale.

Mary put a finger to her lips. If the driver got an inkling of their subterfuge, he could put the brakes on the entire journey.

Mary smiled at Percy, then, remembering the men in her family tended to be sullen and serious, readjusted her face into a suitably reflective and philosophical expression.

'Yes, I believe we have much to learn in Switzerland.' She coughed. Her throat was dry and unable to keep up the low, abrasive tone she'd attempted.

Jane looked at her with a nonchalant expression perfectly suited to her masculine attire. She was the very picture of restraint and the absence of amusement.

'The journey is long enough; it will stretch to intolerable lengths if you keep up that painful accent all the way there. The driver is not interested in your playacting; he scarcely cast a glance in our direction. So long as he is paid, and the coach leaves on time and arrives at its destination, that is the sum total of his involvement.'

Suitably berated by Jane's firm tone, Mary and Percy took their seats in the coach. Jane had already taken the opposite seat and had stretched her legs out so that it was impossible for anyone else to take the seat next to her. Mary's cheeks burnt at the impertinence of it, but the chance to be close to Percy, their arms and legs fused together, quickly turned her on to the benefits.

'You really resemble Mr Godwin when you are attired like that...'

'There are many similarities between us,' Mary countered sharply, extinguishing the train of conversation. 'How shall we call our Jane? I think the name Sebastien suits her well?'

'Sebastien!' Percy exclaimed. 'We did not tell her about the Sebastiens at the Filles et la Sottise, did we?'

His attention suitably diverted, Mary rested her head on the side of the carriage, and shortly the roll and rumble of it lulled her to sleep. Percy and Jane's voices ebbed away until they became nothing more than a faint hum.

Suddenly, a piercing noise stabbed at her temples like a shard of ice. She was in a dark, cold cave, an icy wind bouncing off the stone walls and tearing towards her in the shape of a screaming mouth. As it got closer, she could see black eyes in a skeletal face. It was a face she recognised. It was the monster that had haunted her dreams ever since they'd set foot in Paris — it was the face of her conscience: distorted, disfigured and vile.

'Wake up, Mary. They need to change the horses.' Percy shook her gently.

Mary lurched back into consciousness. 'I must have fallen asleep.'

'You kept shouting out *monster*,' Jane tittered, as they descended from the carriage and stretched their legs. 'Dressing as a man is turning your imagination macabre.'

Mary ignored her. 'Where are we?'

'Eight leagues from Paris.' Percy yawned, his face taking on the drawn, waxy, moon-lit pallor that usually accompanied the insomnia of a creative rush of ideas or the agony of too many thoughts swirling around his brain. Travel had been taxing for them all. Mary could not help but wonder how life would have turned out if they had just stayed in London. The very reason for their elopement was to rid themselves of rumours and obstacles, but all they had done was replace them with new ones. 'We are not changing horses again until Neuchâtel, when we will be in Switzerland.'

Mary sighed and rested her head on Percy's shoulder. 'Do you hear that owl in the distance? Tell me, what is he speaking of?'

'He is talking to the weary moon. She has forgotten why she must shine; the owl is reminding her.'

'What does he say, Percy?' Mary snuggled into him.

'The moon says, "I wander wearily, I chase the sun into silence, my pale constancy seeks … something."' He sighed, turning his eyes from the moon back to Mary.

'Back in the *voiture*.' The driver's words were less poetic than Percy's, but every bit as welcome.

Mary found herself once again grateful for the flexibility of her new attire as she climbed back into the carriage, collapsing once more onto the seat opposite Jane.

Jane stretched out. 'I had a lovely dream. I dreamt I met Shakespeare, and we sat on a hill eating apples.'

'How were the apples?' Percy asked.

'Sour and hard.'

'And Shakespeare?'

'Charming.' Jane rubbed her hands together. 'What are our next steps when we land in Switzerland? Where shall we go?'

'We shall ask where people go to be seen and where they go to disappear,' Mary whispered. 'Percy's clever procurement of funds will enable us to move around comfortably.'

'Do consider that a good proportion of funds has been spent on getting us to Switzerland and out of Paris — neither the coach nor the clothes came freely.'

'But just think, Percy,' Jane said, folding her arms in front of her, 'once we are back in our usual garb, you get two more outfits for yourself and we will be returned to our worn-out, unfashionable London dresses. The Paris sun has practically bleached them of all colour.'

'I hardly think that clothes suited to your size and stature will fit mine…'

Mary giggled. 'He is right. Percy is at least half a foot taller than both of us. These pantaloons will scarcely reach his knee.'

'That would be most appealing in this heat,' Percy reasoned. 'Perhaps I can start a new fashion for a shorter pantaloon?'

'A new pantaloon for a new poetic coterie.' Mary clapped her hands together in delight. 'The Don Quixote and Cervantes of Paris!'

Fuelled by conversations of literature and philosophy, they passed the rest of the early morning in an easy reverie and maintained their good mood throughout the day, even though their stops were few and the food disappointing. Mary's paranoia remained steady, but with each new league travelled, she attempted to rationalise the fear, reminding herself of the distance between herself and Paris.

She still hadn't worked out why the woman at the window of Madame Thibeaux's apartment had reacted in the way that she had. Who was she, and what was she doing in Madame Thibeaux's apartment? Mary's mind twisted itself into uncomfortable patterns, trying to work out the scenarios: did someone want to frame her for Madame Lamont's disappearance? Was it more than a disappearance? Why had she been so quick to believe that Madame Thibeaux had left the objects on the table as clues? What if it was nothing more than a coincidence? It was entirely possible that on being introduced to Mary, Madame Thibeaux had been reminded of her mother's greatness and had wanted to immerse herself in Wollstonecraft's words, hence why she had retrieved her book.

What if Mary was taking them all the way to Switzerland for nothing?

Soon, the intermittent greens and arid yellows of the French countryside shifted into more consistent patches of vegetation, the houses outnumbered by trees. All of this went unnoticed by the occupants of the coach, who could only imagine these changes from within the windowless carriage. When they finally stopped to change the horses, Jane was the first to step out of the coach.

'Oh, this is beautiful. Shall we stay here?'

Percy and Mary rolled their eyes.

'Look, there is a lake over there. Are you not tempted to bathe?' Mary asked with a smirk.

'Nothing would give our identity away faster than the shedding of these clothes,' Jane countered.

'She has an excellent point,' Percy said with a laugh. 'You two must stay where you are. I, on the other hand, have no such limitations.'

'Percy...' Mary started, but it was useless; his white buttocks had already leapt out of his clothes and into the water. He splashed up and down merrily. Mary smiled, but a cold dread swept over her, a feeling that this freedom was fleeting.

CHAPTER EIGHTEEN

The border that divided France and Switzerland may as well have been a knife slicing the two countries apart, so stark were the differences between them. Mary marvelled at the small Swiss cottages tucked quietly into the countryside, where their whiteness shone against the lichen greens and even the air smelt sweeter. The stifling heat of Paris was replaced by a refreshingly modest sun, perfectly in keeping with the rest of the environment. Mary and Jane had changed back into their usual clothes and replaced their carriage some time before the border, owing to a prior engagement of the driver. The coach that had followed was superior in every aspect — its main advantage being windows, which enabled the coach's inhabitants to absorb every inch of this fresh landscape.

A certain divinity and piousness pervaded the towns they travelled through, making Mary blush with self-consciousness at how their arrival must seem in such a religious place. High mountains tipped with pine appeared and disappeared between splashes of green and forgotten rocks as the coach rolled on. Percy took her hand, his eyes wide with excitement; this was a golden place for one with an imagination like his, and Mary could practically see the words flying around his head like small birds waiting for a place to land.

'Is this not the most beautiful of all the places we have visited?' he said, almost breathless.

'I think it is the finest place I have ever seen,' Jane answered. 'Perhaps we shall stay here for the rest of the season.'

Mary smiled. If only she had kept a count of all the times and places Jane had uttered those same sentiments; each stop had brought a new fascination for her, even if the fascination had been as temporary as a cloud, a blue sky waiting for the greyness to take over.

'I have learnt much about Switzerland and its people from the writings of William Godwin,' Percy continued.

A sudden chill ran down Mary's spine, reminding her that however far they travelled, they would still, one day, have to return to England and her father's stony silence. Of all the places they had travelled, it echoed loudest here, amongst the perfect symmetry of the houses and the dark majesty of the mountains.

The coach stopped, and the driver made his way towards a cottage on the opposite side of the lane.

'Why have we stopped?' Jane asked.

Mary shrugged. 'I do not know.'

The driver had taken off his hat and was talking to a stout woman holding the whitest linen Mary had ever seen. The woman looked towards the coach, shook her head and then shouted something into the cottage, at which point a man came out, as lean as she was stout, who began talking to the driver.

'I wonder what they are talking about?' Jane said, darting her head back from the window when she caught the eye of the driver.

'Shh, do you hear that?' Percy silenced them. Now that Mary had stopped to listen, she could hear the horse whinnying.

'The horse is hurt,' she said, softly. 'What can we do?'

'Perhaps we should get out of the carriage?' Percy suggested. 'I shall go over to the driver and see what is to be done.'

Mary could not tolerate any animal's distress, and her hand flew up to her mouth.

Jane reached out to her. 'It is all right, Mary. There is nothing to be done. I am sure all the horse needs is a rest and then all will be well again.'

Mary nodded, but Jane's attempts at sympathy did nothing to dampen the fatalistic thoughts that circled her head like a murder of crows. To think that they should be the reason for the horse's discomfort — their desire for travel — was distressing. She closed her eyes, suddenly lightheaded.

'Are you ill? Do you feel faint?'

'I think ... perhaps a glass of water?' Mary murmured, before slipping down into the seat of the carriage. Jane screamed for Percy, who raced back to them. They carried her out and laid her down on the grassy knoll beside the coach.

A small wave splashed her face.

'There she is.' Mary opened her eyes to see the woman from the cottage standing over her. Her pinched features matched her no-nonsense demeanour. The woman nodded, picked up her bucket, and walked back to the cottage.

'I am soaked...' The water made Mary's teeth chatter, but it had brought her back to her senses. The neighing sounds had stopped. 'Where has the horse gone?'

'The horse is having a rest. There is a fresh one coming for us. He will take us to Saint-Sulpice,' Percy replied, kneeling to brush Mary's wet hair off her forehead.

'How far away are we?' Jane asked, biting her lip.

'Not so very far, just a couple of leagues.' Percy put an arm around Mary's shoulder and helped her to her feet; she stood a little unsteadily. 'We shall have food and drink at the cottage, to recover your strength.'

Mary nodded. 'But the horse is well?'

'Quite well,' Percy replied, but the glance that passed between Percy and Jane told Mary it was anything but.

When the new coach arrived an hour later, Mary's health was restored and no further mention of the horse or the driver was made. The new driver was a local man called Gaudenz, who was a picture of orderly efficiency. His carriage was equally tidy, painted a verdant green atop a dazzling white. They passed an exceptionally pleasant journey through to the next town, taking a descent for almost a league between layered rocks which hid behind pine trees and leafy glades. As the carriage moved forward — the pace hastened by the newness of both horse and driver — specks of light brown offered the smallest divergence from the palette of the countryside; these were quickly explained by Gaudenz, who had fashioned himself as something of a local tour guide.

'The glades are the most beautiful you will see anywhere,' he said proudly. 'They provide excellent pasture.'

'And are those cows that graze over there?' Jane asked.

'Yes, they are Pinzgauer; they give the sweetest milk and cheese. Perhaps you will taste some.'

'Is Switzerland a popular place for visitors? Does it attract many people from Paris?' Percy asked.

Mary was shocked at the bluntness of his question and impressed that he'd asked it. She herself had been wondering how to turn the conversation from cows to travellers and potentially missing wives.

'Of course,' Gaudenz answered. 'People come from all over the world to see the Alps; they are a source of great inspiration, as I am sure you can see.' The driver stared at Percy. 'You have something of the poet about you.'

Percy smiled. Mary raised her eyebrows. It pleased her to consider how easily a kind word would soothe Percy's spirit. The idea that he looked like a poet would be enough to convince him of the worth of his travails for many leagues more.

'I write the occasional poem, yes, but I fear no poet will ever surpass Wordsworth's sublime ode to Uri's Lake.'

'It is impossible not to be charmed by Lake Lucerne; it is where all the grand tourists head.'

'And what about the people who do not wish to be seen?' Jane asked.

Mary glared at her, annoyed that Jane had stolen her question. It was her nature to sit back and listen and to make a judgement once in possession of all the information. Once she had reminded herself of that fact, she sat back and waited for Gaudenz's response.

'There are plenty of places to hide,' Gaudenz began, 'but as a man of the light, I know little about them.'

It was clear to Mary that Gaudenz lived a noble and pious existence, undertaken well and simply. He did not seem the kind of man to embroil himself in anything out of the ordinary. Danger to him might be taking a wrong turn on a road or the disappearance of a beloved cow; his existence knew nothing of the cavernous spaces of humanity or the dark desires that lived there.

Church bells chimed from a giant red tower that pierced the sky like a bloodied spike. A meandering path snaked its way around the lake, the brilliant whites and greens rolling on around them in glorious solemnity.

'Now, this is charming,' Jane said, pressing her face against the carriage window. The lake's cerulean splendour reflected the mountains and the sun setting behind them. For Mary, there was something below the surface of the landscape, something at once strange and unsettling, as if the rolling mountains with their black rock and gaudy hints of white were concealing something malevolent. Monsters. Hanging from the rockfaces, swooping across the mountains, chasing the carriage; there were monsters concealed by nature, as if it were lending a hand to their duplicitousness.

'This place is completely untouched by anything but nature's immaculate hand,' Percy murmured, awestruck.

Perhaps the monsters were hers and hers alone.

After Saint-Sulpice, the mountains pierced the sunset more aggressively. Two leagues from Neuchâtel, the Alps came into view, edging their way forward across the horizon, dominating it. Mary had never seen anything as immense or as constant before. The sterility of the landscape which bewitched Percy and Jane made her uneasy, the mountains taking on the judgemental eyes of her father and Mary Jane, their white tips fading into the dying face of her mother. By immersing herself in the art of living, she felt she betrayed the dead, but that was foolish. Her mother's journals had talked just as much of Switzerland as of Paris, but this openness, the harsh whiteness that greeted them, seemed to conceal more darkness than the shadows of Paris. Of all the ghosts she was carrying with her, the desire to uncover the mystery of Madame Lamont's disappearance haunted Mary the most.

'We seem to have exchanged the stifling heat for incessant rain.' Jane sighed, wiping the condensation from the carriage window. The Alps were masked by a summer fog that accompanied the downpour. Their guide had told them they traversed Lake Lucerne, and they had to take his word for it, as nothing more than blurred outlines could be discerned in the distance.

'Let us recite some Tacitus to sharpen our minds, even if the scenery is dulled,' Percy countered, taking out his pocketbook and thumbing it until he landed on a suitable quote. 'Here's one: "Men are more ready to repay an injury than a benefit because gratitude is a burden and revenge a pleasure." What do you think of that statement?'

'Shakespeare's plays would seem to agree with the sentiment,' Jane said. 'I doubt that the average man would have the means or inclination to enact revenge as magnificently as Shakespeare's villains.'

'I think you underestimate their sex, Jane; even the simplest of men might harbour the deepest of feelings. One may never know the passions that stir behind the stillest chest.'

Mary's thoughts were of her own passions, the depth of feeling that Percy had awakened in her, that primitive passion that captured her soul. She would never have entertained their elopement without it. He alone had the power to bewitch — in six years he had already hypnotised two women into eloping with him. It stung Mary to think that she might only be one in a long line of women; she dared not think how many women had succumbed to his soft words and cherubic features over the years. Women fell like petals at the feet of poets; Jane herself harboured an unhealthy obsession with Lord Byron, and she had the temperament that poets wrote sonnets over, not Mary. Her pale face reflected against the abstract landscape of the window confirmed she was nothing special. How long would her features sustain Percy's interest before his attentions were once again diverted by the freshness of a new muse, a new adoration? Nausea crept over her and held her by the throat. Mary coughed it away; it did not do to harbour such thoughts when there was so much to think about.

'Even the bravest are frightened by sudden terrors,' she said, reflecting on her own.

'No one is safe from terrors; neither man nor woman,' Percy said. 'I have heard many ghost stories about the haunting of the lake, Jane. I will recount them when we are safe in our lodgings.'

'And where are we to rest?' Jane asked with a yawn.

'We shall rest at Neuchâtel and consider our next steps.' Percy opened the window and called out, 'How long until Neuchâtel?'

'Two leagues,' was Gaudenz's reply.

Quotes from Tacitus and conversation exhausted, Mary turned her attention once more to the mist outside. It was slowly lifting to reveal the immense Alps along the skyline. The countryside between the towns alternated between forest and rock, and just as they became accustomed to one scene, it was exchanged for a new one. This part of the journey was more tumultuous than the flatter lands, and at various times the coach rocked precariously. Mary's stomach flipped and churned with each undulation, and her relief was immediate when they finally reached their destination and stepped out of the carriage. The hotel before them was perfectly square and looked as if it had been placed in its unusual position alongside the trees by a celestial hand.

Percy advanced to secure lodgings for the evening, but when he returned to the carriage, his face was ashen.

'This has taken nearly all of our money,' he said.

'How can it be so expensive?' Jane raged. 'It is not Paris.'

Percy sighed and brushed a weary hand through his hair. 'We are in their debt; they set their prices.'

'Well, I think it is ridiculous, exploiting travellers like this.' Jane folded her arms. 'I have a good mind to complain.'

'To whom? What good would it do, anyway?' Percy continued. 'I will be away to the bankers in the city in the morning — perhaps there we will have better fortune than we had in Paris.'

Percy took the luggage off the carriage, carrying it over to the hotel with Gaudenz. Once he was out of earshot, Jane leant towards Mary.

'For a rich man, Percy has no money, Mary.'

Mary breathed deeply; she agreed, but knew that no good would come from saying so. Jane was not a person to confide in; she stored up grievances, ready to throw them like weapons whenever they were needed.

'Travel is very expensive, and we have the added expense of an extra room and a third traveller that we had not factored into our original plans.'

'And what is your reward if you find the missing Madame Lamont?' Jane demanded. 'Or have you completely abandoned that scheme?'

'I have not abandoned it.' Mary's cheeks burned. 'But if she does not wish to be found, then she will not be.'

'I do not believe that she would have failed to elope with a man like Frederic Martin. A man like that can make a woman do anything he pleases…' Jane sighed. 'There is no way she would have stayed with Monsieur Lamont when she could have eloped with Frederic. It is impossible.' Jane clearly ranked Monsieur Martin's charms more highly than Mary did. His charisma had seemed little more than an extension of his theatricality — a well-versed performance that would only fool those without experience of genuine love and passion. It was no wonder they had worked so effectively on Jane. Still, they had deflected her affections away from Percy and, for that at least, Mary was grateful.

'There are an additional six Napoleons if we uncover definitive information about Madame Lamont.' Mary shifted the conversation back to its previous topic.

'Do you believe we will find her here?'

'I do not know.' Mary shook her head. 'I did not mean to fall into this detecting. I do not seem to have a talent for it.'

'You do yourself a disservice,' Jane countered. 'You understand people; you have always had an uncanny knack of empathising with everybody. I have every faith that if there is a case to be answered, then you will solve it.'

Mary blinked. That was the kindest thing Jane had ever said to her. She was in half a mind to take out her paper and write it down, immortalising the kindness in her journal for posterity.

Percy appeared. 'Shall we go in?'

The early morning sunrise swept over them, pushing the clouds so low down in the sky that Mary thought if she put a hand up to them, she could touch them. Once the sun had raced through its bright dawn, it left blue and grey footprints behind, and the weather battled to hold off the rain. Breakfast was as light and efficient as everything else, and they ate it quickly and quietly. Percy left to find sponsorship from the bankers, leaving Mary and Jane to walk through the town together.

Mary felt insignificant against the black summits that shadowed the buildings; each comprised a sharp tower that spiked the skyline. Roofs and towers were set into deep triangles or squares, and the cobbled paths provided the only curves. It reminded Mary a little of Troyes, with a similar air of stillness and quiet contentedness with itself that Paris never seemed to master. As well as feeling insignificant, Mary felt self-consciously outside of the local ways; she could not picture herself scrubbing at white steps like the women she passed, nor could she imagine herself dressed head to toe in white, head bowed like a religious statue. *There are plenty of places to hide.* Gaudenz's words echoed in her mind, and she feared it would be impossible to find Madame Lamont.

She tried to put herself in Claudine's shoes; if she had escaped to Switzerland without Frederic Martin, then why had she left? What could she possibly do? A Parisian woman of great wealth would stick out more than one of the church spires. A sudden peal of church bells disturbed a mischief of magpies, who flew out from the church roof, their colour blending and contrasting with the sky at intervals. Was it easier to hide if you blended in? A row of nuns walked past, their heads bowed, hands concealed beneath bell-shaped sleeves. Their slick black habits swished along the pavement as they moved with synchronised devotion.

'I could not imagine devoting my life to the Church.' Jane shivered as they walked past.

'It is a life of simple devotion and devoted simplicity,' Mary countered. 'I can see why it would appeal to the pious.'

'Have we not devoted our lives to philosophy? To Percy's vision of utopia?'

Mary rolled her eyes. Utopia. The manmade kind. Mercifully, Harriet had not answered Percy's rash letter, inviting her to join them in their utopian society. He was in the habit of sending them; the first had been written not long after Mary and Percy's acquaintance began in May, and the second one had been more of a request for her to bring them some money — beautifully worded so the financial request was a secondary matter. Mary had learned quickly to allow Percy to indulge his fancies. There was no sense in denying them; they rarely came to fruition. When he had first suggested that Harriet join them, Mary had made no comment on the proposal's merits or failures, hoping that it would be little more than another of Percy's whims — a half-baked plan to assuage his guilt over leaving Harriet behind. Mary wondered how Harriet's pregnancy was advancing. Had Percy's letter even asked her about that? She shook her head. It did not do to dwell too much on what they had left behind, or who. The important thing was to move forward, always to move forward.

'Jane, did Frederic Martin tell you when he started his relationship with Madame Lamont?'

'I do not wish to think of it,' Jane snapped.

'Come now, you are hardly expecting a letter of intention or a marriage proposal, are you? You have spent but one night together.'

'Love is not a prison sentence. Emotion is not earned. A true heart will know itself in one night, Mary. You of all people should know that.'

'And what is that supposed to mean?'

'Mama's letters are full of the scandal you have left in your wake, the rumours that swirl around about your name, how you and Percy had to leave because of your adventures on your mother's grave.' Jane smirked.

'And what do you know about any *adventures* on my mother's grave? What possible *adventures* are even to be had on a grave?'

'Well, *you*, if the rumours are to be believed.'

Mary felt her ire rise. She gritted her teeth and balled her fists.

'You take that back! What an abominable thing to say.'

'It is not what *I* am saying, it is what society is saying.'

Before she knew it, Mary's hands were in Jane's hair, pulling her back until they both landed on the cobbles in a flurry of flying hands and kicking legs. They hardly noticed that a crowd of people had gathered around them. Two of the figures in black broke away from the crowd, pulling Mary and Jane apart.

'Ladies, nothing will be solved with violence.' A stern face cast sharp glances from within a black hood.

Mary and Jane turned their eyes to the ground. Embarrassment doused their fury. Neither spoke. Another voice broke the silence.

'What has passed in my absence?' It was Percy.

With a small cry, Jane ran quickly into Percy's arms. Percy, who had been holding some canvas bags, dropped them and accepted her with one arm, the other stretched towards Mary, his expression one of bewilderment.

'Oh, Percy, I have never encountered such violence from anybody; I should never have expected it of my sister.'

Jane's shoulders convulsed, long, loud sobs followed. Percy raised an eyebrow at Mary, who shrugged her shoulders and rolled her eyes in response. Jane would do anything to get his attention and to paint her as the villain of the piece. There was little to be gained in adding to the theatricality of the scene. They had caused enough commotion. Mary's distrust of her sister prickled afresh like a re-opened wound. It could only be healed by her return to England. Mary cursed the fact they had talked her into staying. She would talk to Percy about Jane's immediate return.

'There were no letters for us at the *bureau de poste* and it will be a week before their next delivery,' Percy said, extracting himself from Jane.

Jane's red eyes locked with Mary's, a smile of smug satisfaction on her lips. Mary was tired of these games; she had no intention of being part of any utopia which involved Jane. In fact, she would go so far as to say that she could be part of no utopia which would welcome Jane's admittance.

Percy's voice drifted back into focus; she hadn't been paying attention to what he'd been saying, but whatever it was, it had turned his expression from discomfort to disbelief.

'I'm sorry, Percy, can you say that again?'

'I said I can scarcely believe it.' Percy shook his head. 'The banker has advanced so many coins, I barely had pockets or bags enough to carry them.'

Percy distributed the canvas bags to Mary and Jane, who clutched them tightly.

'Of course, these écus will have the same fate as the francs and louis d'ors we have carried. They will be gone before we can say Jack Robinson.'

Mary put her arm around his shoulder. 'Now, Percy, do not be melancholy. You are the saviour of our little expedition. Thanks to your enterprise and social standing, we will eat, rest and have adventures. Our names and bearing bring nothing but scandal to our endeavour, and it is you and you alone who funds it.'

Percy kissed Mary on the cheek, all good humour restored.

'Let us away. We must find somewhere to stay!' Percy rallied. Together they walked down the path, Percy's arm around Mary, his other linked through Jane's. Mary knew the nuns were watching them; one even drew a sign of the cross with her finger as they passed by. For a moment, she envied their devotion and its absolute absence of a material desire. Her devotion to Percy was disorienting, constantly throwing up new obstacles that she could never have imagined. It would be easier to worship him as an ideal rather than a flesh-and-blood man; no one felt threatened by another's pious devotion. It was passion that turned people into monsters, not love.

CHAPTER NINETEEN

Another three days passed in endless travel. Even the mountains seemed to merge into one, their stately magnificence becoming an overbearing shadow hammering against the windows of the coach like the rain that had fallen incessantly since they'd stepped into the carriage.

Mary closed her eyes to the view, overcome by the sickness that had frequently accompanied her on their voyage. The proximity of their quarters was doing little to improve morale; her head throbbed at the dull, heavy weight of the atmosphere between Percy and Jane, who had been in a quarrel since leaving Saint-Sulpice. It had started with Percy's indelicate attempt at questioning Jane's behaviour, which had led her to throw a shade upon his own. Before long, they had been sniping at each other like a pair of angry birds.

There had been no mention of Madame Lamont for days, and Mary concluded the clues left in Madame Thibeaux's apartment had been nothing more than a trap to throw them off the scent and get them out of Paris. Had someone been lying in wait for their return to the apartment? Someone who'd known that she would be instantly drawn to any and all reminders of her mother, someone who knew who her mother was, who Mary was and where this tangled web would lead? But who could know her so well — or how could she be so easy to read? She felt foolish for galloping away from Paris, and somehow felt sure that the finale of this sorry scene was being played out in that city while they trundled through mountains, imprisoned behind the Alps.

Their behaviour in front of the nuns at Saint-Sulpice had illuminated aspects of her own personality that she did not care for, and any suspicion of Monsieur Lamont being responsible for the disappearance of his wife was now completely erased. His concern for Claudine and his desire to know what had happened to her had appeared genuine. The conjecture that he was standing in the way of some tremendous love affair she was conducting with Monsieur Martin had been little more than a product of Mary's own prejudices. Now that she really came to consider it — and the gnawing pain at her temples crushed all other thoughts out of her head — she realised that part of her wanted to blame the abandoned spouse because of her own guilt over Harriet. Perhaps Madame Lamont, having experienced the passion of a fresh love affair, had decided that she wanted neither life and had the money and the means to escape from both. A woman with money could pay her way anywhere, take on whatever new disguise she wished to — even a life in a nunnery was a possibility. Mary sighed. She would just have to make peace with the fact that she might never have the answer to this question, just as she would never shake the guilt of breaking up Percy's family.

'We must make sure to stop at the Cathedral of St Ursus; it is much praised.' Percy's excited tone broke into Mary's thoughts.

'Cathedral?' Mary replied. So far, the journey had consisted entirely of spikes and spears, the churches disappointingly modern or depressingly archaic, with little to commend them. She felt judgement ringing out with every toll of the bells, castigating her morality with a religious wounding. The thought of visiting another cathedral was almost intolerable.

'Perhaps you might like to take Jane on this adventure,' Mary suggested as she massaged her temples. 'My head aches and I feel unequal to the appreciation of the splendour.'

'Gaudenz, how long to Soleure?' Percy called out to the driver.

'Another hour,' came the reply.

'Then we shall arrive before the sun sets — the cathedral will look most charming against the dusky skyline. Are you sure you cannot be tempted, Mary?'

Mary, who desired nothing more than something to eat, a soft bed, and an escape from the tyranny of her headache, shook her head. When the time came, she was glad of the silence Jane and Percy left in their wake.

'Well, that is a most disagreeable cathedral.' Percy slammed the carriage door shut behind him, stirring Mary from her uneasy slumber. Jane followed quickly, wearing a similarly thunderous look.

'I have no desire to stay here a moment longer.' He smacked the side of the carriage. 'Drive on, Gaudenz. I would rather travel through the night to Lucerne than stay in this intolerable place a moment longer.'

'What happened?' Mary stammered.

'They would not allow me inside the cathedral because they said I was ungodly. *Ungodly!* By what measure do they call me ungodly? By what judgement?'

'Perhaps it is merely our nationality that hinders. Perhaps it was not meant as a personal judgement?'

'They asked if she was my wife...' Percy gestured towards Jane, her arms tightly folded across her chest. 'She said no and that the woman in the carriage ... meaning you...' He paused. 'She said that the woman in the carriage was not my wife, either. That my wife waited for me in England.' Percy slumped back into the coach seat.

Mary's temples throbbed again. The thought of an entire night spent in this strained atmosphere and physical discomfort filled Mary with dread. Despite himself, Percy could be soothed by a good meal, some kindness, and a good night's rest. Separation from Jane would be helpful to them all.

'Let us travel on to the next town, Percy. This constant motion is making me nauseous, and I fear that the threads of our good humour will unravel entirely if we stay in this coach a moment longer than is necessary.'

'Fine.' Percy's mouth was a thin line. 'Gaudenz, drive on to the next town.'

Percy and Jane spent the duration of the journey in silence, avoiding eye contact with one another. Mary, stuck in the middle of this battlefield, could only hope that a ceasefire would be reached at the new town.

'We will get a room of our own, Percy,' she whispered to him. 'And we shall spend the night wrapped in each other's arms and with no thought for the outside world.'

A room of their own they got, but the passionate night Mary had predicted was replaced by dismay and agitation. Everything about the room was wrong, from the broken spinet at the foot of the bed to the large cabinet of stuffed birds perched next to it, their globular eyes fixed in their direction, awaiting entertainment. Even the supper had been meagre and disappointing, and despite Mary's best efforts, there was no change to either Percy's ill humour or to the drilling at her skull.

The night passed in this dissatisfied fug. Though they lay in each other's arms, their physical proximity could not mask the distance between them. Mary's ill health and Percy's malleable moods had hindered what should have been a honeymoon of getting to know each other and, for the first time, Mary harboured doubts about their relationship. Even if they returned to England now, she was tainted with the stain of their elopement, and it would tarnish her character more than his. For a man, it was almost to be admired, but for a woman, unless that relationship proved its worth and was eventually solemnised, then it meant disaster and the end to any hopes of a social life.

Mercifully, the rising sun brought with it an improvement in their spirits, and the coach departed as soon as it could. A brighter morning tempted the mountains into clear sight, and the daylight bathed the countryside in a golden splendour that caused the icy peaks to sparkle and shine. Even Jane seemed brighter than in previous days, and the animosity between her and Percy mellowed into its former politeness. Mary's headache had gone and though a weariness lingered from an almost sleepless night, it held no monopoly against the dazzling horizon that swept away all melancholic thoughts.

They arrived in Lucerne in time for a bounteous breakfast, which they took by the lake, watching the boats sailing upon it. The morning heat bounced off the water, reflecting the white sails of the boats and the cool, icy peaks of the mountains. A brief trip to replenish supplies enabled them to join the people on the lake and they spent the rest of the day serenely watching the landscape roll by from the water. Pine forests and rock decorated the shoreline and the further down the lake they sailed, the more their geniality grew.

'Shall we read some *Histoire du Jacobinisme*?' Mary asked.

Percy, lying back in the boat with his arm outstretched like an oar, smiled back at her, the smile illuminating and casting out all the shadows. Mary's heart fluttered and that invisible thread that bound them together pulled at her, tightening the bond between them.

'Yes, that would be perfect,' he answered.

Mary took the book out of her bag and read, Percy regarding her as if she was hewn from the same ethereal beauty as the landscape. If only he could always look at her that way.

The town of Bessin welcomed them with its slow, sleepy air and they disembarked, shedding more of their coins as they left. Gaudenz met them at the shoreline, waving as he took the luggage from the coach. The harsh lines of the mountains matched the symmetry of the pines that dotted the landscape, as if the mountains were nothing more than the shadows of the trees cast down by the sun. It was evening now and cooler. Mary had been glad of the break from the monotony of the cobbles; the quiet equilibrium of the water had been the perfect antidote. Percy slapped some notes into their driver's hand. It was easy to see how he should shed so much of the stuff; coins ran like water through his fingers. A tight knot formed in her stomach as she foresaw a life of penury and a constant scramble for money. It was not so different to a life with William Godwin, with bailiffs knocking at the door. There had been evenings when Mary's father had gone without an evening meal because he was in his library, too entrenched in sorting out a business deal or the securing of funds to pay yet another red-inked bill. It was money that had first brought Percy into Godwin's favour; he'd been quick to offer financial assistance. Mary had found the letter promising to be Godwin's benefactor and Jane had delighted in recounting the rumours swirling around London that Percy Shelley had paid William Godwin for his daughters' company. Those hateful rumours that had populated Mary Jane's letters to Jane resurfaced in her mind, tightening the knot and spreading the discomfort to her chest.

Percy put his arm around her. 'Gaudenz tells me there are a couple of hotels along here. He has secured our rooms.'

The group made their way along the path, the shoreline quickly joining hands with the forest. Once in the thick of it, the sunlight faded and was replaced by a hazy, green shimmer which cast an emerald light onto the ground, bathing everything in the same glow. It gave Percy an ethereal hue, which made Mary giggle.

'What are you laughing at?' Percy asked.

She smiled. 'The light has turned everything green; it looks strange against your skin.'

'Is it making me monstrous?' Percy boomed, but his voice was too soft to cause any real terror. Even with his hands outstretched, as if ready to grab a victim by the throat, there was not the hardness behind his eyes that really had the power to frighten. Mary's mind flashed back to Scotland, several years earlier, when she had made the charmless acquaintance of her friend Isabel's brother-in-law; now there was a sinister man. Everything about him was solid and strange, with absolutely no tenderness. He had wrought every shred of good humour out of her sweet Isabel, and she shuddered to think of the depth of his influence now she'd heard they were to marry. Of all the games society bid them play, the game of love was truly the most terrifying.

'This cannot be it?' Jane's voice trembled. Mary looked towards where Jane's gaze was directed. A building, half-hidden among the trees, square as a jaw, haunted the landscape in its attempts to be inconspicuous.

Mary frowned. 'What is wrong with it?' She could not see what ailed Jane. 'I am sure it will be admirable.'

Percy grinned. 'Gaudenz will go ahead and secure us the most reasonable rate.'

Mary bit her lip. He could be so gullible sometimes, always trusting people to do his tasks, always assuming that they were as straightforward as he. One of these days he would learn that the world was not like that; some fate would befall him that would crush his idealism in one foul blow. That was not a day to relish.

Mary took Jane by the arm, whisking her around the house to show her that nothing lurked outside it. Up close, there was a greater distance between the forest and the house than they had first realised, as if even the forest had retreated away from it in fear. Mary gulped and hoped that Jane had not seen. She praised each of the aspects they saw, the brightness of the exterior, the clean rows of windows, the alcove above the door at the back. All was precise and ordered, which — as she reminded Jane — was more than could be said of their hotel in Troyes.

'Do you see?' Mary proclaimed, stretching her arms out and striding towards the rear door of the hotel. 'All is perfectly normal.'

Her words were halted by a hastily opened door. A cloaked figure came rushing towards them, looking back into the hotel at the danger they'd left behind. With no thought of the potential perils that lay ahead, the figure careered into Mary's path, and both fell heavily to the floor. Whoever it was, they had trapped themselves in their cloak and wrestled to escape. Mary sat back, watching as the absconder pulled at the fabric until she could see their face. She gasped.

CHAPTER TWENTY

'You!' she cried.

The woman scrambled to stand up, but Mary's grip was strong.

'Jane, fetch Percy and Gaudenz quickly!'

Mercifully, at that moment the figures of Percy and Gaudenz came into view, illuminated by the glow of the lamp Percy was holding out in front of them.

'What is going on, Mary?' he asked, passing the lamp to Gaudenz and rushing to Mary's side.

'Hold her arms,' she said firmly. 'She was trying to escape.'

The woman on the floor had turned her head away from them. Her hair had slipped free of its constraints and pooled behind her.

'I don't understand,' Jane stammered. 'Who is it?'

'Do you not see, Jane? It is Madame Lamont ... or at least, the woman who resembles her.'

'She called herself Pascale,' Percy stammered, his eyes wide.

'But why is she here? And why was she trying to run away?' Jane asked.

'That, Jane, is what I intend to find out.'

'Let me go! You do not realise the danger you are putting us all in!'

Under the harsh glare of the hotel lantern, the woman's face was pinched with fear.

'You are not going anywhere until you tell us who you are and why you are here,' Percy said firmly.

'I believe that you know more about the disappearance of Madame Lamont than you have told us,' Mary added, scanning the woman's face for the resemblance to their quarry. Up close, their similarities were superficial, and this face lacked the kindness of the woman in the portrait. This woman's look was marked by a ferocity of expression which told Mary that she had led a very different life to Madame Lamont. 'Monsieur Lamont is beside himself with worry.'

The woman's lips curled into a sneer. 'I doubt very much that Monsieur Lamont is beside himself with anything other than relief.'

'It is as I thought; you know something of it.' Mary sat back in her chair, folding her arms. 'Perhaps we can take some claret and supper and discuss it in more detail, just you and I?'

Percy shook his head at the proposal. 'Mary, I will not allow it,' he said.

Mary tipped her head to one side. 'Percy, she has no weapon, and she cannot wound me with words.'

'I am not in the habit of harming women.' Their guest spat the words at Percy. 'It is men I do not trust.'

'And probably with good reason. Come along, we will find another space in which we may converse freely.' Mary held out her hand as if picking up a fallen friend. It was accepted. She smiled at the woman, though trepidation made her hands tremble. The hotelier directed them to another room. 'Shall we?'

Mary closed the door behind them. The room was stark and empty, with nothing but a table, chairs, and a row of keys hung from a panel on the wall. Her eyes quickly assessed all the surfaces, looking for potential weapons — anything that she might need to use or might be used against her. Returning her gaze to the woman in front of her, Mary sat down.

'Might we be formally introduced? My name is Mary Wollstonecraft Godwin. How do you do?'

'I am Helene, Helene Pascale.'

'Very well.' Mary cleared her throat, smoothing down her dress with her hands before cupping them together in front of her. 'Now we are introduced, will you tell me what happened to Madame Lamont?'

'I will tell you this: while you stay here, you are in danger … all of you. He will stop at nothing to cover his tracks.'

'Who? Monsieur Lamont?'

'Leave. Go back to England. You are nothing but a pawn in his game. He has killed Madame Thibeaux; you are leading him back to me. He will kill us all.'

Jane entered the room with a carafe of claret, water, bread and cheese. Mary loaded the items onto the table, but Jane loitered. It took three firm gestures before Jane, pouting, reluctantly closed the door behind her. Helene poured out two glasses of wine. Mary watched as she took one and sipped from it.

'I know you are in a hurry to leave, so perhaps you will allow me to offer my summation of events?' Mary picked up a piece of bread and took a bite, swilling it down with claret.

'I am all ears,' Helene replied, sitting back in her chair.

'You worked at the gentleman's club in Paris, Les Filles et la Sottise, where you met Monsieur Lamont, who noted the similarity between you and his wife. Monsieur Lamont had heard a rumour of his wife's relationship with Frederic Martin and their elopement to Switzerland, so he killed her, disposed of the body, and planted you in Troyes to create the impression that Madame Lamont had gone into hiding.'

Helene laughed, clapping her hands together in delight. 'An excellent theory,' she said. 'But tell me one thing: where is the body?'

Mary sighed. 'Now that, I do not know. But I think that you do ... and you are going to show us, unless you want me to inform the gendarmerie of everything we have learned.'

'We are beyond the border; they have no jurisdiction here.' Helene leant forward. 'I like you, Mary. I see that we both have a fighting spirit and a desire for justice. But I can also see that your gown is worn, and the way you ravaged the bread tells me you haven't eaten well in days, so you know how hard it is to be an independent woman without means. I need money, Mary. I want to get as far away from this monstrous tale as I can. Come with me, just you and I, and I will show you where the body is. If you can get the money for our passage, I will tell you everything. What you do with the information after that is up to you.'

Mary got up from the table. 'Leave it with me.'

Percy, Jane and Gaudenz were huddled outside the door, springing away from it as Mary turned the handle.

'Must you stand so near to the door?' she chided.

'Your safety is my paramount concern, Mary,' said Percy, rushing to kiss her. 'I cannot stand the separation.'

'Well, you must endure it a while longer, Percy. Helene has confessed to her part in Madame Lamont's death.'

'Death?' Jane gasped, clutching her chest.

'I fear so,' Mary continued. 'She will tell me everything, but there are conditions — both hers and mine. She asks that we pay for her passage to Germany and offer some financial incentive. I ask that you and Jane follow on the next boat behind us and from Germany we go back to England. I am tired of all this running around.'

'Gaudenz will make arrangements,' said Percy, nodding at the driver. 'How much money does she require? I have … er … just recently committed to a house by the lake.'

'Percy!' Mary cried. 'We have only just arrived! How have you secured a house in that time?' She closed her eyes and took a deep breath. 'No matter. Can you not retrieve your funds?'

'No, I am afraid they have gone already. Is there no way we could uncover the truth and return here, rather than going back to London?'

'I think that once the truth is unveiled, we will need to be as far from this sorry story as possible.'

CHAPTER TWENTY-ONE

The moonlight made monsters of the trees; the branches stretched out like gnarled hands, the twisted fingers primed to grip the necks of unwary travellers. The moon's luminescence bounced along the glacial mountaintops, chasing them like an angry phantom as the carriage moved on. Helene sat mutely in the carriage, next to Jane, who threw occasional sidewards glances at her. Mary's eyes met Helene's. She tried her best to smile, but she knew it could not hide her distrust, the unshakeable feeling that she was walking into a trap and might never get out. Her mind whirled with the possibilities, unfurling and tossing themselves before her like discarded leaves.

Madame Lamont was almost certainly dead. She had not been seen or heard of since her husband had returned from Troyes. Helene had somehow played a part, but what? Mary surveyed Helene's outfit, the trousers, shirt, coat and cap designed to alter her appearance and make her look like a man. Two women travelling alone on a boat would be too great an attraction to be ignored.

Gaudenz gave Mary the tickets and guarded Helene as Mary said her goodbyes.

'Are you sure you want to do this?' Percy's voice was weak, and his eyes shone with tears. 'You should not be alone with her. I do not trust her.'

'You do not need to trust *her*.' Mary kissed him. 'You need to trust me. I will wait in Mannheim at the port for your arrival. Will you wave goodbye?' She struggled to keep the emotion from her voice, instead drowning out her own words by enveloping him in a long embrace.

'We do not want to miss the boat,' Helene said.

Mary and Percy looked at each other, affection running deeply between them. Mary put an arm on Jane's shoulder.

'Take care of yourself and take care of Percy. I will see you over the Rhine.'

As soon as Mary and Helene boarded the boat, the smell of vomit hit her nostrils and turned her stomach. They showed their tickets to a disinterested man who was trying to prevent a fight between two drunken men. Mary took Helene's arm, as if her masculine attire might deflect attention away from them.

'We need to find a changing room.' Helene's eyes darted around the boat, looking for a space that was not taken up by rowdy men. 'Here, come on.'

'What are we doing?' Mary asked, as Helene took her by the hand and pulled her along.

'I am showing you exactly how easy it is to become someone else.'

Minutes later, they returned to the deck, dressed in each other's clothes. It was the second time on this trip that Mary had worn trousers to conceal her true identity.

'Look at your reflection.' Helene walked them over to a window where they could see their reflections. 'Do we look so different from one another? Watch.'

Mary inhaled sharply. Helene, in Mary's outfit, had got it all — the quickness of her pace, the slight dip of her shoulders, the downward turn of her gaze when she did not want to look or be looked at; all her mannerisms were showcased in front of her.

'How do you do that?'

'I am an actress, remember.' Helene shrugged. 'My profession is to watch and mimic people.'

'But that's me ... that's me,' Mary stammered, struggling to respond to the mirror image of herself in front of her. Ordinarily, there was but the scantest of similarities between them.

'It's uncanny.' Percy's eyes widened then darted from Mary to Helene. 'But where did you see Mary?'

Helene shrugged. 'While you were looking for her, I was watching you.'

'I must leave, the boat is about to depart.' Percy's voice trailed behind him, Mary watched him go but was distracted by her thoughts rushing to make sense of it all.

'*You* are the missing actress from the gentleman's club?' A piece of the puzzle slotted into place for Mary. 'Where you met Monsieur Lamont?'

'Correct,' Helene said flatly.

'You were in a relationship with him,' said Mary, with dawning comprehension. 'He convinced you to be a part of his plan to murder his wife, because you could impersonate her?'

'Yes.' Helene smiled. 'That was one of the major attractions of the club and one of its greatest ironies. Men came for the company of other women, but in reality wanted little more than women who could mimic their wives.'

'But you went missing in March, and Madame Lamont did not go missing until July?'

Helene laughed. 'Are you sure of the timeline, Mary, or is that merely what Monsieur Lamont told you?'

Mary rubbed her forehead, pushing her cap up. 'You're saying that Claudine Lamont went missing before July?'

Mary's head swam. Suddenly her body felt weightless, as though there was no substance to it at all. She struggled to hold herself up and tried for words, but nothing came out. Then she passed out.

When Mary awoke, she was on the empty top deck of the boat, looking up to the night sky, a welcome breeze on her face.

'Has that been happening a lot?' Helene asked.

'Do not tell me you are a nurse *and* an actress?'

'An actress must be all things…' Helene pointed at Mary's stomach. 'And see all things.'

'I have not bled these past two months,' Mary whispered. 'I thought at first it was the sickness of the journey, but now I am sure that it is not.'

'Does your husband know?'

'Percy is someone else's husband,' Mary whispered. 'But our souls are married and that is enough for now. His wife, Harriet, is to have a child soon. How can I tell him that mine will shortly follow?'

'Soon you will be unable to disguise it.'

'I know.' Mary shook her head. 'But we are not here to talk about me. We are here for you to tell me what happened to Madame Lamont.'

A rustling sound told Mary they weren't alone. A boatman stepped towards them. Mary squinted. The face shadowed by the brim of the dark cap was familiar. It was Monsieur Lamont.

Mary's heart thudded as he approached her.

'Did you know that if a body is thrown into these waters, it is almost impossible to find?' His voice was loud, with no hint of emotion. 'And sometimes,' he continued, reaching into his pocket, 'the only way to identify a drowning is through a personal item, something that belonged to the deceased.' From his pocket he pulled out a copy of Mary's mother's book, *Letters Written in Sweden, Norway and Denmark.* Mary frowned, realisation dawning that this was the same book she had seen in Madame Thibeaux's apartment.

'It was you! You planted those items on the table!'

'You did not really think that meddlesome old woman was trying to help you, did you? She is old and forgetful, but also Claudine's closest confidante and the only other person I needed to get rid of. All I needed was a gullible person to blame for the murder I was going to commit, and you, Mary, are that person.' He began ripping pages from the book, paper fluttering at his feet and occasionally taking to the air like birds before crashing down into the water. 'I hoped that you would believe the woman you saw in Troyes was my wife and you would testify that with the police, but when you had your doubts, I needed to make another plan. Then I hoped that you being found at the apartment of Madame Thibeaux would be sure sign of your guilt, but you did not go to the police. When you did eventually go back, I had paid the housemaid to tell me of your return; I had people waiting to call the gendarmes the second you arrived. That should have been enough to get you imprisoned and get rid of you, but I underestimated your ability to run … and your resourcefulness.' He sighed; the book collapsed at the spine, falling limp in his hand. 'But really, I cannot thank you enough. You have sniffed out and devoured every morsel I have left for you like a mouse following a trap but, as we know, it is only the second mouse that gets the cheese and now…' He threw the book into the water.

Mary struggled to get up, but the deck was slick. Helene strode over to Monsieur Lamont, cupped his face in her hands and kissed him slowly. As she did so, she pulled a gun from his pocket and pointed it at Mary.

'All I needed were your clothes; now I believe you will play the part of Madame Lamont. Is that not so, my dear?' Helene inclined her head towards Monsieur Lamont, but kept the gun pointed at Mary.

Monsieur Lamont nodded. 'The world believes that she planned to elope with that playwright... What was his name again, my dearest?'

'Frederic, my love. What a sweet little cuckold he was.'

'You killed Madame Thibeaux!' exclaimed Mary.

'Madame Thibeaux need not have died, but she started scratching around, sending her cook to Troyes, telling anyone who would listen that Madame Lamont had not been herself lately.'

'And she had not,' Helene laughed. 'She had been ... *me*. Should we confess the entire story to Mary, now that she is to take Claudine's place in the Rhine?'

'Very well. A confession will give some absolution, and then a swift resolution of the situation will allow us to start our new life in England, as we planned.'

Mary thought she saw a flicker of hesitancy in Helene's eye as Monsieur Lamont said this.

'Helene and I met at the start of the year at the gentlemen's club. It is important for a man to have hobbies, do you not agree, Mary?' Monsieur Lamont leant over the railing, closed his eyes and breathed in the night air. 'Claudine has never been an exciting or sociable woman. Apart from her altruistic concerns and the garden, she has very little interest in anything else. Helene lit up my world like a firework; she brought me back to life when I had not even realised I was dead.' He coughed before continuing. 'I saw how well she impersonated people, so I took Claudine on a brief trip to Troyes ... and put

Helene in her place in Paris, just to see how convincing she could be.'

'You told us that Claudine had never been to Troyes,' Mary interjected.

'Ah, well, at the time I wanted you to think that. Helene had been in Paris in her place, you see, so there could not be reports of Claudine being in two places at once, if the deception was to work.' He coughed again.

'Are you well, my love? Perhaps take a drink. Do you have a hipflask with you?'

'No, I do not.' He attempted to clear his throat.

'Here, have some of mine.' Helene passed him her hipflask, a flash of metal reflecting against the barrel of the gun. 'I will continue with the story.' She looked at Mary. 'I masqueraded as Madame Lamont for a week or two, but I was doing so well that Pierre made the arrangement permanent. I had an affair with Frederic Martin; after that, it was easy to sow the seeds of a woman on the verge of casting off her old life and starting again.'

'If Claudine had been as devoted as you, my dear, there would have been no need to kill her,' said Monsieur Lamont, taking another sip from the hipflask.

'Let me get this straight,' Mary said, struggling to keep up. 'If you had been playing the part of Madame Lamont since March, what had you done with Claudine?'

'She never came back from Troyes,' Helene said simply. 'But a week after her disappearance, I boarded this boat as a man and left it as a woman, making my way back to Troyes until the coast was clear.'

'You see, there are always people who can be bought,' Lamont continued. 'Your entire journey has been populated with our puppets — pulling your strings whilst driving your horses, giving you money, sending you notes. I have mapped out your journey so precisely that I am thinking of becoming a cartographer.'

Lamont and Helene laughed uproariously.

'You have seen how people behave on this boat: drunks, brawlers … people in disguise. No one pays any attention to who gets on or off, as long as they are paid.' Lamont shrugged.

'You mean, Madame Lamont was thrown overboard and left to drown?' Mary's voice quivered.

'Precisely. I knew you were intelligent. A child of Mary Wollstonecraft — how could you be anything else? I drugged her first to make sure she was quiet.'

'You will hang for what you have done, for the crimes that you have committed.'

'But Mary,' Lamont said, 'you are the only one to hear our confession. You and the moon, and I do not think the moon is likely to tell tales now, do you?'

A monstrous gurgle followed his words. Monsieur Lamont clutched at his throat, his skin flushing purple. 'Helene?' he mouthed, his voice hoarse. He fell to the floor, his movements jagged and desperate like a fish out of water. His hands pawed at his throat until his fingernails ripped through the skin, leaving angry red lines. Mary stared, paralysed with fear, before a cry left her own mouth.

'Help him!' she shouted, jumping to her feet and rushing forward, retreating as the cold barrel of the gun reminded her to keep her distance.

Helene shook her head. 'It is too late for that. He is dead. Give me your cap.'

Mary took off the cap. Helene took the bullets out of the gun and put the gun in the cap. Then she grunted as she pushed the body over the side. It landed in the water with an enormous splash.

Out of nowhere Percy and Jane ran up to them. 'Is someone going to tell me what has happened?' Percy asked.

'You're on the boat?' Mary croaked, staring at them with wide eyes. 'You were both here all the time? Even when I had a gun pointing at my stomach?'

'Oh, hush,' Helene said, as if calming a tantrum. 'You were never in any danger, but I needed to make it appear as if you were in order to get Pierre to trust me enough to...' She trailed off.

'Enough to what?' Percy asked.

Helene shrugged. 'Enough to kill him.'

CHAPTER TWENTY-TWO

Mary exhaled deeply; the Rhine's calm surface revealed none of the murky secrets that lay beneath it.

When the previous night they had alerted the boatsmen to the drunken man who had fallen off the boat, their report had been met with the customary shrug and a half-baked promise that they would send a boat after first light to look for him. It had not stopped the boat from continuing in its quest to reach Mettingen.

'Will you tell us the rest of the story now, Helene?' said Mary, once they had disembarked. 'Now that you have killed Monsieur Lamont?'

'I did not kill Monsieur Lamont,' Helene corrected. 'He killed himself. That hipflask contained the poisoned liquid that he intended to use to kill his wife.'

'Intended?' Jane asked with a frown. 'There are more twists and turns to this case than in a novel by Ann Radcliffe. I simply cannot keep up with it all.'

Helene nodded. 'I understand, and I will tell you all once we reach Gernsheim. Until then, you must be patient.'

Jane sighed. 'Then I think I might read some Rousseau; I shall sit on that grassy bank over there.'

'A capital idea,' Percy said. Jane walked away, watched by the others.

Percy turned to Helene. 'How do you learn the mannerisms of another person?' he asked. 'If, for example, you were impersonating me, how would you do it? What qualities would you heighten?'

'You walk like a duck, and you trip over your words,' Helene replied immediately, scrutinising his face as she spoke. Mary tried to stifle her laughter. 'If you cannot find an expression, or the continuation of an idea, you look up to the heavens as if you could retrieve it from there.'

'She is right, Percy. It is your poetic disposition.' Mary smiled. 'Of course, we do not need to hear of my mannerisms, for I have already had a most accurate display of them.'

'And Jane's?' Percy whispered. 'What about hers?'

'She has a fierce, determined walk, as if she is being bolstered along by a sudden gust of wind.'

'You would not believe it now,' Mary countered, looking over at her stepsister, an unexpected contentment passing over her. 'She seems most engrossed in the book.'

'I have been writing a romance in our journal, Mary. It is inspired by you. Perhaps you will read it on the journey back to England.'

'That would be splendid, Percy, but first we are to go with Helene to Gernsheim and conclude this story — is that not so?'

Helene nodded. 'It is, and once it is resolved, I shall return to Paris and tell the gendarmerie of all that has passed — well, perhaps not all.'

They boarded the barge and headed in separate directions. Percy and Mary sat in the quiet tranquillity of the top deck, while Jane and Helene took a stroll along the lower deck.

'I cannot believe that the only part of this story that Monsieur Lamont did not orchestrate was Napoleon the donkey and my twisted ankle.' Percy sighed. Mary squeezed his hand, knowing that talk of the absent donkey was difficult for him. Percy had always had a love of animals.

'I am sure we will see Napoleon again one day, but if we do not, then at least we know he is well and being cared for.'

'Yes, Mary, that is true.' Percy kissed her hand. 'I am sorry I did not protect you from Monsieur Lamont. I feel I have been nothing but a tremendous disappointment to you. Thank goodness Helene secured tickets for myself and Jane for this journey and arranged our safe passage without your eagle-eyed detection. We have been in disguise too…' Percy sounded very pleased with himself; Mary did not have the heart to tell him she would have recognised him in a heartbeat if she'd seen him earlier.

She clasped his hand; she was going to need him more than ever in the next few months. Their bond would be tested and strengthened by the baby growing quietly in her womb. For a moment, she thought about telling him.

'Tell me one of your poems,' she said instead, closing her eyes, the waves lulling her into a gentle sleep as Percy's words danced across them.

Several hours later, the barge stopped at Gernsheim, and they walked along cobbled streets and countryside that divided earth and sky more evenly than Switzerland's landscape. There was something reassuring to Mary about the absence of the overlapping sky and mountains of the Alps. It was easier to see the sun, and it shone upon them with divine clarity, warming her through, soothing away all thoughts of the previous night. The only imposition on the landscape was a castle that clung to the top of a hill, surrounded by stone pillars that cast unfriendly shadows on the pavement in front of it.

'Have you heard the story of Castle Frankenstein?' Helene asked.

Mary felt a sudden chill, as if icy fingers had caressed her shoulders, and pulled her shawl around her. 'I have not,' she replied.

'Oh, it is truly a magnificent place. Let me see if we can access the grounds. I would tell you the story myself, but I think it is much better to hear it from a local villager.'

The villager happy to tell them the story was a short man with a slight stoop and a hooded eye that he closed for dramatic effect. He told them of the alchemist Konrad Dippel, who had lived over a century earlier. He had devoted his life to the study of bringing the dead back to life. Mary, who had spent a lifetime immersing herself in her mother's works, listened with fascination to the tale.

'How did he get the body parts?' she asked breathlessly.

'It is rumoured that he dug up the graves, ground the bones to dust and mixed them with blood.' The villager's eyes were wide.

'I do not believe it.' Jane sniffed, turning her face away from the castle. 'There is no way of bringing the dead back to life.'

'You do not think so?' Helene asked.

'No. Once someone is dead, they stay dead —' Her words were cut off by the figure of a ghost stepping out of the castle's shadows. A woman, dressed simply but elegantly in a loose blue gown, removed the scarf from her head, revealing neat hair in the sculpted style of Parisian high fashion. She glided towards them gracefully, making Jane grab onto Mary's arm.

The woman reached out to Helene, who embraced her warmly.

'Is it over?' the woman asked.

Helene nodded. 'It is over.'

Mary gasped. The two women could have been twins, or at least sisters. As they wrapped their arms around each other, the resemblance was striking. It was easy to see how Helene had fooled Claudine Lamont's friends and acquaintances.

'Allow me to introduce myself,' the woman said, stepping forward. 'I am Claudine Lamont.'

'You are alive,' Mary whispered. 'Thank goodness. Have you been here all this time?'

'This is not my castle; I have been staying here with friends while Helene sorted out the situation.'

'What, the situation in which your husband kills you and then you wait until he's dead to come back to life again?' Jane said with disbelief.

'Yes,' Claudine said simply. Her hand went to the soft curve of her stomach, which had been well disguised by the flowing fabric of her dress. Mary's hand went to her own stomach. They had more in common than she'd realised. 'Please, come inside.'

The castle was old and draughty, the wind whistling through the gaps between the windows. A suit of armour outside a door made Mary jump and almost knock it over, apologising as she rushed to stabilise it.

'Helene, can you make refreshments while I seat our guests in the drawing room?' said Claudine.

The room was grand and plain. Military artefacts populated its stone walls; flickering candles made the shadows in the corners dance. It was clearly a room that never saw daylight, a perfect place in which to hide away from the world. Mary pulled her scarf around her. Percy watched her, a growing suspicion clouding his expression. She dared not look at Jane.

Claudine rubbed her hands together. 'I was delighted when Helene told me that none other than Mary Wollstonecraft's daughter and the poet Percy Shelley were investigating my disappearance.'

Jane coughed. 'I helped too.'

'Apologies. I do not know your name…'

'I am Claire… I mean, I am Jane Clairmont.'

'It is very nice to meet you, and I must thank you all for freeing me from that monster. You must tell me everything that has happened.'

Mary told Claudine of their adventures since arriving in Paris, including their involvement with Monsieur Lamont, Madame Thibeaux and Frederic Martin. Claudine listened intently, putting a hand to her heart at the mention of Madame Thibeaux's death and nodding with a curious detachment at the re-telling of a romance she had never taken part in. Helene returned with a tray of refreshments; she poured the tea without asking and handed one to Mary, who nursed it on her knee.

'Well, pleasantries concluded, I am sure you have questions you wish to ask?'

'I have one,' Percy started. 'If you were poisoned and pushed off a boat, how can you be sitting here now?'

Claudine smiled and winked. 'Never underestimate the power of women working together. Wouldn't you agree, Mary?'

'I agree most wholeheartedly, but I must echo Percy's sentiments. If Monsieur Lamont poisoned you with the same poison that has now killed him, how did it kill him and not you?'

'Perhaps I may answer that,' Helene interjected. Claudine gestured for her to proceed. 'You are familiar with the tale of Romeo and Juliet? Where Juliet appears to be dead, but the effects of the poison are in fact only temporary?' Helene put down her tea and took a vial out of her pocket. She shook it and tiny black seeds stuck to the side of the vial like insects.

'Opium. The dose was enough to dull Pierre's senses, but not enough to kill him. He took that before we even got on the boat. He was always a nervous traveller. He hated travel by road and insisted on boats, however out of the way they took us. The boat on that fateful night was taking us to Creteil; there's an island there. I knew he had something planned, but he didn't know that I had a plan of my own. He was planning to get off at the island and take the next boat back to Paris, pretending we had gone to Troyes, then Switzerland. It was to be quite the adventure.'

Mary's mind flashed back to the men on the boat, how impossible it would be to spot the drugged from the drunk. How easily a man could be one thing or the other. For the lower classes, nasty assumptions of character would be made that money would cushion the upper classes from.

'So, when he wanted us to investigate his missing wife, you really were missing? He did not know if you had fallen in the water — as he'd hoped — or made your way to safety? Presumably, when he awoke and found you missing, he assumed his plan had been successful?'

Claudine shrugged. 'Yes, presumably, but we will never know. I cannot swim far; he knows — knew — that. But it is done now, and he is gone.'

A sudden chill descended; Mary wrapped her arms around herself. The night air could be cruellest in summer. Or was it the subject matter that was making her feel the cold?

'You acted as though you'd been poisoned, just long enough for his poison to kick in?'

'Quite so.' Claudine nodded. 'I left no trace of myself. I got off the boat in exactly the manner he'd hoped I would.'

If her pregnancy had been anything like Mary's, then her nausea and sickness would have easily fooled her husband into believing she had been poisoned. Monsieur Lamont was arrogant enough to believe in the foolproof conclusion of any plan he had concocted. As for the relationship between Monsieur Lamont and Helene, well, that was easier for Mary to understand. Monsieur Lamont had been fooled by Helene's acting, just as surely as she had fooled everyone else around her in her various guises. It wasn't hard to see that he had been in love with her, as blinded by lust as by his greed and desire to be rid of his wife.

'I tipped myself over the side, then I swam to a boat that was waiting for me.' Claudine breathed deeply. 'Pierre has been trying to get rid of me for years, but I have evaded him with long trips to the country and my own pursuits. It is only since the war and the failure of some of his ventures that he saw fit to redouble his efforts to get hold of my personal fortune. Once I realised it was not only *my* life that was at stake, well, I knew I had to die.'

Mary could picture it now, a dark night in which the river was as black as ink. A small boat could easily hide alongside the shadow of a packet steamer or a barge.

Mary frowned. 'But who was in the other boat?'

'My loyal lover.' Claudine smiled, her face lighting up as she spoke. 'Come in, Patrice.'

Mary's jaw dropped as the grumpy gardener walked into the room, kissed Claudine on the cheek and took her hand. She smiled at him warmly.

'You might recognise our gardener, Patrice.'

'I thought he hated you!' Jane cried.

'Helene may mimic, but I am exceptional at concealment,' Patrice replied, his face breaking into the first smile they had seen from him. The look that passed between him and

Madame Lamont was one of love and devotion. This was clearly not a new attachment.

Mary blinked; another part of the puzzle was falling into place. Now that she saw them together, she could see they were a natural fit. She was embarrassed that she had taken his defensiveness and unwillingness to talk at face value. If only she had dug a little deeper, then she might have seen through his hostility and found the affection for Madame Lamont that lay beneath it.

'My father worked for Claudine's parents as a gardener,' said Patrice. 'We lived in a small cottage on their grounds. There was no way they would ever let us be together. So, I went away and joined the navy, but was discharged due to injury. When I came back, just over a year ago, our feelings had not changed, even though the circumstances had. And now, we are finally free to marry.'

'What about you, Helene? We know how you came to be involved with Monsieur Lamont, but how did you dream up this scheme with Claudine?' Percy asked.

'Claudine showed me a great kindness when I first came to Paris. The help that she and Madame Thibeaux gave me … that kindness demands lifelong loyalty. Pierre paid no attention to her charity work, so there was no way for him to know that we had already met. When he put his scheme to me, I went straight to Claudine.'

'And I saw a way for everyone to get what they wanted.' Claudine shrugged. 'Now that he is dead, I can wait here until the baby is born and then return to Paris. Patrice will return before me, bringing news that I am alive and had gone into hiding, having feared that my husband was trying to kill me. Helene will inform the gendarmerie that Pierre learnt of my address and tried to kill me off, again…'

Mary was struggling to keep up: Claudine's tale made her and Percy's elopement seem dull in comparison.

'It is highly regrettable that Madame Thibeaux suffered for it,' Claudine continued with a sigh. 'I was very sorry to hear of her loss, but my husband's fear of discovery was the very thing that enabled this new plan to take shape.'

'What do you mean?' asked Mary.

'Madame Thibeaux was the only person who would not be fooled by Helene's performance. She was a loyal friend who knew me well — though not well enough to know about Patrice. Now, we are free.'

Mary gulped. 'You have told us freely and plainly of your plan and the methods you employed to undertake it. Why would you tell us all this if not...?'

'Do you mean to kill us all?' Jane interjected. 'Are we to be imprisoned in this castle, never to escape?'

Claudine laughed. 'No, of course not! Pierre killed Madame Thibeaux, so he would have hanged for his crime. We have expedited his demise, that is all. Other than that, there is no call to answer. Do you not agree?'

'Absolutely!' Jane clapped her hands together. 'Now, if I remember correctly, the boat is to depart soon, so if there is nothing else, I think we should be going.' She went to rise, but Mary pulled her back down.

'And what will you do now?' she asked.

'We shall stay here for the rest of the summer, before Patrice goes back to Paris with the news of my reappearance. I'll join him shortly after that. Helene is to return to Paris sooner, to declare herself to Frederic and try to win his heart with her own charms.'

'It is regrettable that I had to go to Troyes, but in order to play the part of Madame Lamont and protect Claudine, I had to go through with Pierre's plan.'

Jane's eyes flashed. Mary bit her lip. Jane would not appreciate any competition for Frederic's affections, even if she had only secured them temporarily.

'I would seek affection elsewhere, Helene,' Mary said simply. 'Frederic has been neither loyal nor abstentious in your absence.'

Helene simply shrugged. 'He is a free man; he must do as a free man will.'

Mary saw Percy's eyes light up. She rolled her eyes, predicting what would come next.

'You are welcome to join us in our quest to create a new utopia,' Percy started. 'We are determined to bring together the disciplines of philosophy, poetry and affection to quash the social restrictions of matrimony, religion and monogamy.'

'Come along now, Percy,' said Mary, rising to her feet, 'you have writing to do. Utopia will have to wait until you've completed your next collection.'

Claudine stood too. 'Before you go, may I give you something? A token of my appreciation?'

Claudine disappeared from the room. The sounds of doors closing and footsteps scurrying made Mary think of the legendary alchemist dragging the bodies to his laboratory. It was a relief to see Claudine reappear in the doorway with three small boxes.

'Withdrawing money would have alerted suspicion, so instead I have spent years investing in jewellery, just in case I should ever need to secure funds quickly.'

'You predicted your husband would try to kill you?' Jane stammered.

Claudine laughed, handing her a box. 'No, of course not, but as a married woman all my money goes — went — to my husband. Jewellery is a lot easier to fence.'

'Can I ask about that?' Jane continued. 'When we looked around your bedroom, there were very few personal possessions. Where did you keep your jewels?'

Claudine tapped a finger against her nose. 'I cannot tell you that, but I can give you this.' She handed a box to Jane.

Jane's eyes sparkled, their shimmer almost matching the brilliant blue sapphire that dangled from the necklace she held in her hands. As Jane twirled it around, the sapphire cut through the gloom, casting blue teardrops of light on the stone walls. It was the most beautiful thing Mary had ever seen, and the most decadent too.

'Is this really for me?' Jane asked, gripping the necklace so tightly that Mary thought Claudine would have to wrestle it back from her if it was not.

'It is. Now, this is for you, Percy.'

The box Claudine handed to Percy was long and thin. He slid it open, revealing an ornate, gold pocket watch infinitely superior to the one he had sold to finance their travels. Its reflected light infused his disbelieving face with a golden glow, which warmed Mary's heart to see.

'And let us not forget Mary, dear Mary.'

Mary did not enjoy being the centre of attention, nor the knowledge that their investigation had perhaps saved one life but ended two others. She vowed never to take on a detecting case again.

'I really do not need any jewellery or —' Mary's words were swept away by the sight that greeted her when she opened the box. It was a bracelet comprising two rows of gold links connected by brilliant diamonds, pearls like small moons, and emeralds that brought to mind the lush greens of Lake Lucerne. 'It is staggering.' She snapped the case shut. 'It is far too much. I cannot accept it. We cannot accept these gifts. Percy, Jane, hand them back.'

Percy and Jane looked at each other, deflated. Slowly, they too went to hand the boxes back.

Claudine shook her head and folded her arms. 'Please, do not insult me by giving them back. You have done me a great service; you have given me the chance of a new life and a great love. I have no need of them or anything else. Please take them, with my very best wishes and thanks. Now, you must hurry or you will miss the barge.'

Helene hugged Mary, Jane and Percy in turn.

'It has been lovely to meet you all. Mary, take good care of yourself. I hope our paths will cross again one day,' she said, as if they'd spent the day promenading rather than solving a mystery.

Together they stepped out of the castle and made their way back to the shoreline, just in time for the barge's departure. Castle Frankenstein watched from the hill, a slow dusk bleeding red behind it. Mary put a hand to her stomach and instantly felt calm. When she turned away, she saw Jane watching her with a look of satisfaction and curiosity.

As the barge pulled away, Mary closed her eyes, keen to leave all the madness behind and sail back to England, into a brighter future.

EPILOGUE

'I have secured a captain for the last part of our journey,' Percy said with a yawn from inside their latest carriage.

They had been travelling for so long that the days and countries had blurred into one another. Once they left Gernsheim and resumed their journey, bad weather and delays at Maassluis had detained them in the port town for more days than they would care to mention. Travel had taken its toll on them all, yet secrecy weighed heavier on Mary's spirit. Jane had guessed at her pregnant state when confronted with her mirror image in Madame Lamont, but Mary still hadn't plucked up the courage to tell Percy about the baby.

It was a blessing that the perpetual morning sickness had abated, but she could not forget that the baby was inside her, growing and gaining strength whilst she felt drained. Once she could no longer blame the boats or the constant motion of carriages for her fatigue, she would have to confess everything.

Mary was still bitter that the elopement had not furnished her and Percy with the time alone that she had craved. Jane's presence had been like a toothache; it did not hurt all the time, but when it flared up, she wanted nothing more than to extract Jane from the situation. She feared she would feel the same way about a baby. After the birth, there would always be three of them, and there was no way that her father and Mary Jane would accept a baby out of wedlock. In matters of morality, Mr Godwin could be old-fashioned, no matter how much he wrote about and advocated for freedom and liberty. Percy would be the father of three children by two women in the space of three years, yet they had lived from hand to mouth, lurching from one financial disaster to another. In London, where temptations were many but friends were few, Mary would be a social outcast with no one but Percy and Jane to turn to. The idea that she would depend on Jane for anything twisted her stomach.

Fear of abandonment tormented her thoughts and haunted her dreams. She foresaw a future which echoed the past, a solitary future in which she had nothing to hold but her baby, her own confinement diverting Percy's affections away from her, just as they had drifted towards her during Harriet's second pregnancy.

Mary nodded to Percy, closed her eyes, and settled back under the blanket. If she could not sleep, at least she could hope for some rest. They would wake her when it was time to depart. At least this way, she could clarify her thoughts and consider the most appropriate time to tell Percy the news. Perhaps she was underestimating him. Their love was not in question, and if they could survive six weeks with Jane, a donkey and a missing person investigation, then surely they could weather an additional member to their utopian society. Such welcome thoughts enabled her to dream, and instead of picturing a lonely, friendless future, she filled her thoughts with a child's laughter, kisses and light. It would be a daughter. She felt certain of it. She would call her Mary, and she would have all her own mother Mary's fire and beauty and Percy's sensitivity and poetic soul. Mary felt less qualified to judge her own contributions, but there were such rich pickings from their heritage that it scarcely seemed to matter.

Her mind played through a scene in which a girl, only three years old, was picking out shells from a golden beach, the hot sand melting between her fingers. The girl's gentle laughter danced upon the air and seagulls bowed and swerved towards her, desperate to join in with the carousing.

At the end of the beach, where the shoreline met the sea, stood a rocky verge, slinking back from the shore as if it did not wish to be seen. But its blackness stood out against the golds and greens as surely as the mountains in Lucerne. A figure emerged, a man with a priestly bearing concealed beneath a long, black cloak. He beckoned the child, who regarded him silently, tilting her head to get a better look. When the child looked up at the sky again, it was black. Though she did not mean to, she ran towards the figure.

Mary appeared in her own dream, soaked with sweat and clutching her chest to catch her breath. Inky fog crawled into her nostrils, filling her lungs. She swatted it away; it turned into a colony of bats, circling her until dizziness overwhelmed her. She found herself in a cave, with a dark pool and a body. Mary picked up the body, carried it to a rock outside the verge, and watched as a single bolt of lightning fired it back to life.

'Mary?' She jolted awake. 'We have arrived.' Percy smiled at her. Mary stumbled as she navigated her way onto the boat, paying scant attention as they exchanged one mode of transport for another.

'Do you have the journal, Percy?' she asked.

He shook his head. 'No, Jane has it presently. I have another one I purchased in Troyes; would you like that one?'

Mary extracted a pencil from her bag, chewed it for a moment, and then began. She scratched the word HATE on the top of the page, underlining it so heavily the pencil broke through to the other side of the paper. She knew exactly what sort of story she would write: a tale of humanity and brutality, and how passions and pursuing power could mar a man's sensibilities. It would tell the tale of the Lamonts and the unbelievable world they had been thrust into, far more incredible than anything she could ever imagine.

She tapped the pencil against her chin, waiting for the right words to form in her mind before setting them on the page. An alternative vision, in which Madame Lamont and Helene simply exchanged places, would be the place to start. After all, hadn't both their stories been as equally fuelled by hate as by love? Helene did not trust men and the unknown, yet doubtless horrible circumstances that had led her to the gentlemen's club. Mary thought back to the way Helene had pointed the gun towards her. Imagine if she had killed Mary, then killed Monsieur Lamont and Claudine, and strolled back into Madame Lamont's life as if it had been hers all along? How easy she had made it seem; how easy to fool everyone.

Mary struggled to keep up with the words, tearing through pages as if possessed by a sudden force, a need to get the words down before they evaporated from her mind. It was the first time she had truly felt creative.

Percy, inspired by her productivity, joined in, adding meat to the bones of the poems he had started in Paris and Troyes. Jane sat quietly, devouring Rousseau's *La Nouvelle Héloïse*, pausing now and then to put down the book and sigh theatrically, before shaking her head and resuming her reading. Moments of equilibrium like this might have convinced Mary that they could live harmoniously together, if she had not been too engrossed in her own writing to see it.

When they reached Gravesend Reach, Mary closed the journal on her story and steeled herself. Percy and Jane put down their books and pencils and joined Mary at the railing, the seagulls welcoming them back to English soil with loud squawks. Jane smiled at a figure on the harbour. Mary and Percy shaded their eyes to see where she was waving.

'It is Mama!' Jane exclaimed. 'Is it not delightful that she should come to welcome us back?'

Mary knew full well that Mary Jane had come only to reclaim her daughter, that she had no desire to welcome Mary back into the Godwin household. She looked beyond her stepmother's shadow, wondering if she might find her father there; perhaps their time apart had reminded him only of his love for his daughter, not his disapproval of her choices and behaviour. There was nothing behind the shadow, no sign of any change in his feelings. Mary's heart sank, but a small fluttering sensation in her stomach reminded her that she would no longer be truly alone. She rested her hand there gratefully, holding her bag in front of it lest Mary Jane's watchful eyes should uncover the truth before Percy.

Jane rushed off the boat and into her mother's open arms. Mary Jane accepted her daughter but trained her eyes on Mary and Percy, who were on the receiving end of a look so black that it could turn day to night.

'Ever since you wrote to me from Germany, I have been scouring the Traveller's Companions and all the routes from Germany to England. I have been like a bloodhound on the scent of your trail.'

Mary picked up the unfriendly undercurrent of the comment, the barely contained disapproval straining Mary Jane's voice.

'How is my father? Fanny?' Mary tried to infuse her voice with as much cheery politeness as she could muster. It was quickly deflated.

'Fanny is most displeased with you. As for the rest of us … well.' Mary Jane huffed, allowing the rest of the sentence to float off into the air.

'I feel you will find us all much changed after our adventures. I have so much to tell you, Mama,' Jane enthused. 'It has been an education in every sense of the word.'

'You can tell us all about it at home.' Mary Jane ushered Jane away, leaving Percy and Mary with their luggage.

'Are Percy and Mary not coming with us?' Jane stopped and looked back.

'No, we are to stand on our own two feet,' Mary replied, taking Percy's hand firmly in her own.

'Oh, well, that is decided then. I am not going home either.' Jane folded her arms.

Mary Jane pouted. 'Do not make a scene, Jane. They are ostracised from moral society, but for you there is still a chance of redemption.'

'I do not wish to be redeemed; I wish to be free.' Jane held her head high. 'And I do not wish to go by the name you foisted upon me; I wish to be known by my own name. From now on, my name is Claire Clairmont.'

Percy's eyes were as wide as his smile of approval. Mary's approval was slower in coming. She knew that now Jane — Claire — had publicly declared herself to be a disciple of his utopian society, they would be dutybound to honour her place within it and keep her with them, even though they had little money and even scanter prospects. Mary feared that the pocket watch and the gorgeous bracelet would be the next sacrifices to Percy's vision.

'Capital.' Percy clapped his hands. 'Capital!'

'And is there not some news you wish to declare, Mary?' Claire's gaze burned until Mary's whole body was ablaze.

'Oh, for goodness' sake,' Mary Jane tutted. 'You're pregnant, aren't you?'

'Is it true, Mary?' asked Percy.

She nodded. Percy swept her up and whirled her around. The motion was dizzying; it reminded her of the ship. Claire was staring directly at her, with such an unreadable look upon her face that it made Mary uneasy. She let out the tears that had stifled her voice, trying to make them appear as though they were tears of joy, not anger and sorrow. She would never forgive Claire for telling Percy and Mary Jane like this and confirming Mary Jane's notion that Mary was the ringleader of this scheme. Somehow, Claire had yet again come out of it innocent and unscathed. It would not always be so, she told herself. It could not always be so.

Mary vowed she would protect the baby growing inside her, whatever the future held. She drew her shawl around her shoulders, rested her hand on her stomach, and closed her eyes. Words floated like clouds before her eyes and Mary sang quietly to her unborn child:

'May howling winds solemnise my vow,

That I shall love you always

As of now.'

A NOTE TO THE READER

Firstly, many thanks to you for choosing to come with me on the first part of Mary Shelley's adventures! It has been a great honour to work with Sapere Books to bring Mary Shelley centre stage as her life can often get neglected because of the tremendous success of *Frankenstein*. She is a fascinating person and was a trailblazing woman with tremendous resilience and grit.

My road to Mary Shelley was an unusual one and came first through learning about her famous mother, Mary Wollstonecraft, and the tale of Mary's birth, then, as a Gothic teenager, I learnt of the romance between Mary and Percy and the rumoured loss of her virginity on (or at) her mother's grave; it was only after learning about her as a person that I came to learn about her as a writer.

I have tried to be as accurate with Mary and Percy's relationship as possible and have sought opportunities to blend fact and fiction as the story dictates. It is well documented that Mary did not particularly want her stepsister coming along with her and that her guilt at leaving her other sister Fanny behind was significant and something she came to. Mary's stepmother Mary Jane Godwin is a combination of invention, speculation, and biographical detail and though she is not in the book for very long, she makes quite an impression, and I hope to get to come back to her again. The spectre of Harriet, Percy Shelley's first wife, who he abandoned when she was pregnant with their second child to go off with Mary, looms large in the tale and Percy did write to Harriet inviting her to be part of their

'Utopia' and to ask for money. Percy Shelley may well have been a genius, but he was not good with money.

The wonderful thing about writing is you get to go on the journey with the characters and Mary Shelley's *History of a Six Weeks' Tour* gives both the timescale for the novel and its picturesque backdrop. Research has yielded some of the names of streets, towns, and cities that they visited in the summer of 1814 and the letters of Mary Shelley, Percy Shelley and Claire Clairmont have also been fascinating points for specific detail. The name of the theatre is fictitious, though influenced by existing theatres such as the Theatre Feydeau and except for the main protagonists, character names are fictious, but the Parisian monikers are inspired by the people I met on various French exchange trips over the years. The use of the term "Sebastienne" is a term given to the city's residents during this time, though the additional context of the name was shaped to fit the demands of the story.

Napoleon the donkey is one of my favourite characters (I like to include animals in my work, wherever possible!) and Percy did buy an ass and then a mule before starting on their journey; I've given the donkey a more prominent role and, I hope, a happier ending in the French countryside than the real animals Percy discarded.

My lifelong fascination with Mary's story made her a natural candidate for a detective series and the timespan of her relationship with Percy Shelley provided an irresistible backdrop. Their burgeoning romance and elopement are well documented, but it has been great fun to imagine a life within the blank spaces and to put Mary, Percy, and Jane at the centre of a murder mystery in Paris. I have tried to imagine her life within the gaps of that period and bring to life the experience of travelling as a sixteen-year-old girl full of optimism, adventure, and love. Obviously, Mary is carrying another passenger on the way back to England in September and book two will continue the journey!

If you enjoyed *The Missing Wife* and would feel comfortable leaving a review on **Amazon** or **Goodreads** that would be greatly appreciated. I hope you have enjoyed your adventure with Mary and Percy and come back to follow them on their next adventure in London!

Sapere Books is an exciting new publisher of brilliant fiction and popular history.

To find out more about our latest releases and our monthly bargain books visit our website:
saperebooks.com

Printed in Great Britain
by Amazon

63299337R00139